OMENỤKỌ

OMENỤKỌ

by

PITA NWANA

First Published in Igbo Language by
Longmans, Green & Co, Ltd., London, 1933

Translated into English by

ERNEST EMENYONU

AFRICAN HERITAGE PRESS
NEW YORK   LAGOS   LONDON
2014

AFRICAN HERITAGE PRESS

Translated Edition, African Heritage Press, 2014

Library of Congress catalog number: 2014952077

Cover Artist: Salem Djebili

ISBN: 9781940729176

ACKNOWLEDGEMENT

I am grateful to the Office of Research, University of Michigan-Flint for a research grant (RCAC) that enabled me do archival research in England, July 7–August 14, 2013.

—Ernest Emenyonu

CONTENTS

TRANSLATOR'S FOREWORD

Pita Nwana (about 1881–Sept. 5, 1968) was the first person to publish a novel in Igbo language. His novel, *Omenụkọ*, was published in London in 1933 after it had won an all-African literary contest in indigenous African languages organized by the International Institute of Languages and Cultures. It is a biographical novel based on actual events in the life of the hero Omenụkọ (real name: Igwegbe Odum) whose home in Okigwe, Eastern Nigeria, was a popular spot for field trips by students in schools and colleges, as well as a favorite attraction for tourists in the decades before and after the Nigerian Independence in 1960.

Generations of Igbo children began their reading in Igbo with *Omenụkọ*, and those who did not have the opportunity to go to school still read *Omenụkọ* in their homes or at adult education centers. Omenụkọ was a legendary figure and his 'sayings' became part of the Igbo speech repertoire that young adults were expected to acquire. The novel has been reprinted several times in various Igbo orthographies and is today, a classic in Igbo literature.

Omenụkọ is in the same category as two other novels in African languages which are not only African classics today, but also like *Omenụkọ*, marked the beginnings of the novel in the languages in which they were published. They are: *Chaka (Shaka)* by Thomas Mofolo (Dec. 22, 1876–Sept. 8, 1948) published in Sesotho language in 1931, and *Ogboji Ode ninu Igbo Irunmale* by D. O. Fagunwa (1903–Dec. 9, 1963) published in Yoruba language in 1938. *Chaka*, a fictionalized story of the founder of the Zulu empire early in the 19th century, was translated into English by Daniel P. Kunene in 1981. *Ogboji Ode*…, a mythical tale was translated into English as *The Forest of a Thousand Daemons: A Hunter's Saga* in 1968 by Wole Soyinka. These three novels in African languages: (*Chaka* 1931; *Omenuko* 1933; *Ogboji Ode*…1938) are widely acknowledged as the earliest novels published in any African language, and are, therefore, the beginnings of the African Language Novel (ALN). Of these three historic classics, *Omenuko* is the only one till now, not published as a book in the English language. This English translation of *Omenuko* was originally done as part of my doctoral dissertation—"The Development of Modern Igbo Fiction…1857–1966"—at the University of Wisconsin, Madison, 1972.

The translation was done for two main reasons. The first is to make *Omenuko* accessible to a global readership. The second is to establish Pita Nwana as the founder and father of the Igbo Language Novel (ILN). The Igbo language novel has come a long way since the publication of *Omenuko* almost a century ago. It suffered decades of setbacks due to overwhelming disputes and unending controversies over which orthography to write in. At times, the imbroglios resulted in serious, even if unintended, roadblocks that threatened the very existence of, and interest, in Igbo language studies and culture. At other times, they crossed the boundaries of healthy intellectual debate and discourse, and turned into personal acrimonies between diverse camps of Igbo linguists each holding rigidly to its different persuasions and ideologies. All these notwithstanding, over one hundred novels have been published in Igbo language since its debut in 1933. The novel, *Omenuko*, shows where and how it all began.

May, 2014

OMENỤKỌ

PROLOGUE
The Story of the Life of Omenụkọ
As Told by Pita Nwana

From time immemorial, in our part of Africa it is almost like an unwritten law that a man does not forsake his fatherland. He can live in a foreign land but no matter how successful he becomes there in business or social relationships, and no matter for how long or how many people among whom he lives hold him in high esteem, there are bound to be things which will remind him once in a while that he is, after all, a stranger there. Whenever there is a mocking reference to this fact of his status in a foreign land, whether by allusion or indirect hint, his desire to return to his homeland becomes a burning issue for him.

This is a very strong belief. Therefore, if anybody provokes the stranger in such a situation, he automatically packs his possessions and goes back home. He is likely to be accorded a hero's welcome by his people and this will more than compensate for all the humiliations and contempt he might have suffered in the foreign land. Eventually he would apply the knowledge and experiences which he acquired in the foreign land towards the improvement of his home town. His achievements would continue to be a source of joy to him and he would always see the truth in the saying that 'East or West, North or South, there is indeed no place like home.' Dear reader, this is what the story of the man Omenụkọ, that follows, is all about.

CHAPTER ONE
The Early Life of Omenụkọ as a Trader

Omenụkọ was the first of a family of six, comprising four boys and two girls. His parents were poor in every respect. They had neither money nor a yam barn to sustain the family. They had no assurance of future livelihood for their children. Consequently, they sent them to wealthy merchants whom they served, and who in return taught them the art of trading. As a little boy, Omenụkọ was apprenticed to a well-known merchant called Omemgboji, in whose service he remained till he matured into a man. At that point, his Master gave him some capital to establish his own trade in appreciation of Omenụkọ's faithful services to him. Omenụkọ was very happy and thanked him profusely. He knelt down and his Master Omemgboji blessed him saying, "I wish you long life and prosperity. May your servants serve you as faithfully as you have served me. Good Luck."

Omenụkọ did not immediately set up on his own as a trader. Rather he attached himself to his Master and ordered his goods through him because his capital was then not big enough for him to set up entirely on his own. He continued in this way until he acquired a sizeable capital and then broke away from Omemgboji and established his own business as a long-distance trader. He had only one apprentice at this time but soon his business grew and within a year a few other apprentices had joined him. They were carriers whose work was to carry his goods to distant lands for sale, and then carry home what goods Omenụkọ would buy for sale at the local markets in his town. Omenụkọ's trade progressed and he was steadily becoming rich. This did not escape the notice of his neighbors who increasingly sent their children to him to be taught trading the same way that Omenụkọ had been taught by Omemgboji.

Omenụkọ's trade involved traveling very long distances. His carriers and apprentices carried his goods walking several days until they reached the market places. They would set off early in the morning and walk for several hours, stopping only for a brief refreshment or a night rest. On one such trip, they passed several nights on the way due to unforeseen circumstances. The first town where they rested for the night was Umuduru Nso Ofo. The next day they reached Umu Lolo and on the third day they reached Ezi Nnachi. On this third day, there was very heavy rainfall which further slowed down their movement and then forced them to halt the journey. When they continued, the effect of the terrible rainfall was evident everywhere. When they reached River Igwu, which was usually crossed by a foot bridge, they discovered that the bridge was hardly visible. The rain had swollen up the river and it was overflowing at every point. Omenụkọ and his team managed to feel their way to the bridge and began to cross. When all of them had gained a foothold on the bridge, the ropes at the edges gave way and the bridge collapsed sending Omenụkọ and his men deep down into the river. Providence was on their side and they all swam to safety. No one drowned because every child in the town was taught how to swim very early in life. Even Omenụkọ's wife who was in the group swam to safety—despite all odds. Unfortunately, however, their goods were not as lucky; they all perished! The river was known for its falls and great rapids such that any object which fell into it was within seconds, swept off and carried swiftly away. That was how all the goods carried by Omenụkọ's men were totally lost in a twinkling of an eye, including all his life's savings in cash which he was carrying to buy goods with. Omenụkọ was thus reduced to wretchedness and abject poverty. He moaned his fate and sobbed bitterly. These were his words: "God Almighty, why have you reduced me to a life where death would by far, have been a better choice?" All passers-by and fellow merchants sympathized and wept for him.

Omenuko and his men returned to Ezi Nnachi, for Omenuko to reflect on what next to do. Here everybody sympathized with and wept for him. Incidentally, the news of Omenuko's losses did not reach home because of the great distance between his hometown and the place of the accident. Nobody had an idea how depressed Omenuko felt deep inside him or what he planned to do next.

After a while, Omenuko gathered all his apprentices and addressed them saying: "If we go back home empty-handed without reaching the market for which we had set out, it would be a shame and almost an abomination to our ancestors and great God on high." He went on: "Please bear with me and have courage so that we can continue to our final destination. There is one secret which I learned from my great master Omemgboji." He told them the story of a famous merchant called Akpo who was from Itu. On one of his major trips across Anyim—the big ocean—his boat capsized and he lost all his goods. Nevertheless, he was not discouraged but continued to his final destination. That made all the difference eventually for him. His business turned out to be a huge success.

This convinced them and they continued on their long journey. They were at this time, a day behind the traders who had passed them on the way when they halted; they equally arrived a day late at the big market in Bende. However, these traders who arrived in Bende before Omenuko's team told the tale of Omenuko's losses. Furthermore, they made it known that Omenuko was not likely to buy goods in large quantities for his return journey as he had lost all his cash. Therefore, he was not going to stay long in Bende as was his custom, before going back. On the same night that his team arrived in Bende, Omenuko visited his friends who were slave dealers and told them that he had brought some "goods" which must be disposed of that very night. He told them of how his goods had perished at the river "except a few." His friends were touched and consoled him saying "if you had not brought so many goods from the start, what could have been your fate now?" They referred to his apprentices as "goods!" "How could you have told this tale?" they asked him. Omenụkọ agreed that he would have been finished completely. They bargained with Omenụkọ and he sold to them all his apprentices and a few of his carriers including one of his cousins, Obioha.

None of the apprentices knew what Omenụkọ had done and they did not suspect him when he called them together and addressed them saying: "One of my friends here, Oji, has been very kind and sympathetic towards me. He said that it would be a great shame for all of us to go back home empty-handed. On his advice, therefore, I am taking home with me tonight only a few carriers, while the rest of you, under the leadership of my cousin Obioha, will stay another three days so that my friend Oji will buy some goods which you will carry home for me to cling on to, till my affairs improve."

After this, he bought as many things as possible with the money which the slave dealers had paid him, and left for home with a few of the unsold carriers, leaving behind him all the others that he had sold to the slave dealers. He warned those travelling with him that they would have to make the homeward journey in half the normal time because he was indeed sorrowful and longed to get back home. But on the way home, Omenụkọ remained inwardly depressed by his recent action, wondering what he would do about the people he had sold and how he would face their parents. His conscience blamed him for ever selling them because what happened to him could not be blamed on his fellow human beings. It was something between him and his God. At night fall they arrived home.

CHAPTER TWO
What Omenụkọ Did on Reaching Home

Nobody at home had yet heard what happened because no one else from the market had reached home except Omenụkọ and his tiny group. No one, therefore, knew about the loss of Omenụkọ's goods at the river or the fate of his other carriers and apprentices "left" in Bende. Shortly after his return that night, he sent one of his younger brothers to the families of the young men he had sold, inviting the parents to his house early the next morning so that he could explain to them what led to his early return when every other merchant was still on the way. He asked his messenger to urge them not to fail to come under any circumstances, because as the saying goes: "The toad never runs in the day time unless something is after its life."

When his brother delivered this message, some of the parents became so anxious and worried that they decided to see him that very night in case he might be kind enough just to give them a hint of what the meeting in the morning would be about. When they met Omenụkọ, they told him that his unprecedented early return had been a source of concern to many people and they were anxious and hoped all was well with him. He briefly explained to them that he would be going back the following day after he had seen a few people that he needed to see at home. He could not afford to stay longer than the next day because his apprentices and carriers were still in Bende waiting for him to get back. After saying that, he requested them to go home because he was tired and needed some rest. When they left he mocked them saying 'people who rush into a battle little realize that war is death'!

Later he called his brothers Okorafo and Nwabueze omitting the third who was too young to participate in serious family discussions. He asked them in a rather bleak manner: 'Supposing I sold into slavery my carriers and apprentices, what consequences would I have to face in life?' His brothers recoiled and answered: "That would be a thing unheard of in our land. Any ear that hears it will tingle. It would be an abomination against our gods and ancestors." His mood frightened them. He then told them what he had been through in his journey, his losses and what he had done in effect with his carriers and apprentices. He declared:"My ancestors and the gods have put me in a condition of life worse than death. I must die. You must therefore, prepare each of you, to fend for himself. I am going to die," His brothers were terrified and asked him,: "Are you saying you will kill yourself?" He replied "Yes, I have to, and as for you, you must each begin to look for a means of sustaining life, by your own efforts." Unafraid of him anymore, his brothers though younger, blamed him severely for his rash act, because, "it is a crime which can never be forgotten in life." They wondered how he could summon up courage to sell the children of not just his fellow men, but his neighbors and relations merely because his goods fell into a river. "Was it the fault of your carriers and apprentices or their parents that you lost your goods?" He admitted to them that he had nobody to blame for his losses. He advised them to make arrangements for their future because he was contemplating an act worse than the selling of other people's children. When his brothers persisted, he revealed to them that he had invited the chiefs of the land and the parents of the young men he sold, to meet with him early the next morning. His plan was that all the chiefs and parents of the young men would die at the same time with him. When they had all assembled, he would set on fire two barrels of gun powder which he had been storing in his bed room. That way, everybody in the building would be burnt to death. That was why he was warning them early enough as his brothers to plan for their safety. His brothers were horrified and began to shout at him ignoring his gesture for them to keep their voices down. They yelled at him: "Never!", shaking their heads in strong disapproval. "You cannot do this. What you have done already defies human utterance. It is a crime that will haunt our family generation after generation till the end of time. Is that not enough harm? Are you contemplating worse than that? Never! Rather than do that, let us flee the land. Our custom allows that. That is the best thing we can do in this situation, because till the end of time we are finished in this land and if we survive the scandal at all, we will remain outcasts forever and ever. This is what our ancestors describe as abomination that time can neither heal nor erase. It stays in our lineage from generation to generation. Our children will have to suffer for it and our children's children will likewise suffer for it for no fault of their own."

Omenuko was deeply touched and persuaded by these words. Together he and his two brothers decided that they must flee their homeland to a town called Mgborogwu. It had always been the custom of their people that when anyone did anything which was an abomination to the land, the person could go into exile among the people of Mgborogwu. In the same way, fleeing criminals from Mgborogwu always took refuge in Omenuko's town. This custom began from time immemorial and no one could explain its origin or the reasons behind it. It had simply lived down in history and was known among the people as "Iri mgbalata" (ritual flight into safety; a kind of reciprocal returning to an otherwise one's home where he/she is accepted unintentionally) and it was honored and respected by the two communities.

Thus, Omenuko and his brothers decided to seek refuge in the court of the ruler of Mgborogwu, himself called Chief Mgborogwu. After this resolution they went to bed and woke up in time to receive the chiefs, elders and parents whom Omenuko had invited early in the morning. When the guests arrived, Omenụkọ served them water to wash their hands and faces. After that customary ritual, he presented them kola nuts and a bowl of clay chalk (nzu) saying: "It is a sad story for me to tell you that I lost all my goods at the Igwa river." He told them how he had lost all his possessions but assured them that he was in a hurry to go back to Ezi Nnachi. He was anxious to mount a search especially now that the high tides had abated and the river was no longer as over-flooded as it was before. He hoped by the help of Chukwu, the great god on high, and his ancestors, that perhaps he would at least recover his guns if nothing else. He further told them that by the time he returned to Ezi Nnachi, his carriers and apprentices would have arrived out there from Bende with the goods which his friend Oji was sending along to help him begin life again. They would then all come back home to nurse their wounds.

All the people who heard his story deeply sympathized with him. When his guests left, Omenụkọ called together his brothers again to work out a definite plan for their escape. They set the hour that very night. His married sister also came home that day when she heard the news of her brother's losses, but when she was told about the other crime committed by Omenụkọ, she trembled and wept. Her brothers acquainted her with their plan for escape and urged her to join them. She consented to flee the land with them because she realized that what her brother Omenụkọ had done would never be forgotten in the land. When they had thus resolved, they urged everyone to take only the most essential things and await nightfall. They could not be saddled with cumbersome load.

CHAPTER THREE
Omenụkọ and His Family Flee their Homeland

That night, Omenụkọ's family acted like people who were going to bed early. They closed their gate so that no visitors might come in. When they believed that everybody else had gone to bed, they sent Nwabueze, one of the younger brothers, to go down the main road out of their town and watch carefully who passed him by or what sounds he heard. When he came back, he reported that he heard nothing and he saw no one along the road. "I heard no sound not even the cry of crickets. The only noise I heard was the screaming of Ibe Ofo." Ibe Ofo was a lunatic who was chained and confined to a cell. His cries and curses could be heard from miles away.

When Nwabueze finished his report, they opened their gate again and made ready to depart. They agreed on how to take along only their own little children safely and noiselessly. When they were all set, they began their exit. They paused briefly in front of what used to be their father's house, now inherited by Omenụkọ as the first son. There was sorrow in their hearts as they took one last look at the house and then left the compound. They set off for Mgborogwu and until they had left their town behind them, they never met a soul on the road. The skies were dark and rain was threatening and when they had travelled about seven miles later it started to rain cats and dogs.

In the morning, cries were heard in Omenụkọ's compound. They were from children that Omenụkọ and his people had left behind. They were the children of their neighbors who were staying with them. When they woke up and looked around, they found no one else in the compound. They were frightened and began to cry. People who heard them from the nearby compounds, stopped by to find out what was wrong. When they noticed the emptiness of the houses, they asked the children the whereabouts of the owners of the house. The kids crying, answered that they had no idea where they were.

The neighbors looked around everywhere but found no trace of Omenụkọ and the rest of the family. They raised an alarm calling on people to come over to Omenụkọ's house and see things for themselves. Within a short time many people had gathered in the compound. They realized that Omenụkọ and his brothers must have fled the town. So they appointed some young men to trace their route and pursue them. When the young men came back late in the evening, they informed the people that they had heard gun salutes coming from the direction of Mgborogwu. The elders, therefore, sent out another set of young men to go and verify if Omenụkọ and his brothers had fled to Mgborogwu. When the young men returned, they confirmed that, and further added that Omenụkọ and his people had taken refuge at the palace of the ruler of Mgborogwu. The Chief and his people had welcomed them happily with a twenty-one gun salute, and had been celebrating with festivities and merriments. They were very pleased because Omenụkọ had a very large family, and was known to be affluent and very generous to neighbors.

Omenụkọ had three wives. Two of them had each a son and a daughter. His next brother Okoroafo had two wives, one of them had a son. His brother Nwabueze was married but his wife had not borne any child yet. They were also accompanied by their youngest brother, their two sisters and their mother. The chief of Mgborogwu was very happy about their number.

The news of Omenụkọ's flight caused a considerable stir in the town. From then onwards people became increasingly worried about the young men who had accompanied Omenuko to Bende and who had not come back yet. Their families, therefore, appointed a delegation of strong men to go and investigate the whereabouts of Omenuko's apprentices and carriers he had left supposedly in Bende. The few carriers who came back with Omenuko told of how he had advised those he was leaving behind to wait for three days so that they could carry home the goods which his friend Oji would buy for him. This explanation did not however, stop the investigation, so the men set out for Bende. After four days, they sent back word from Bende that Mazi Oji had disclosed to them that Omenuko sold the young men as slaves to him.

When the town's people heard these words, that Omenuko did in fact sell his carriers and apprentices into slavery, they were extremely shocked. There were some families who were too devastated to weep for the loss of their loved ones. Others sobbed unceasingly. The tears which were shed in the whole town that day were enough to form a river. The parents of the young men wept bitterly but tears alone could not bring back their sons. Omenuko, himself, felt no better. He had fled from the land and taken refuge in a strange town to live the life of a stranger. His neighbors though, missed him and were sorrowful, but those alone could not bring Omenuko back to them or reverse the crime he committed. He had actually planned to kill himself but his brothers had dissuaded him from that because the manner of the death he chose was not acceptable to them, for it would have brought a curse on the entire family till the end of time. It is the sort of crime that wipes out a whole lineage. Their flight into Mgborogwu, therefore, was the better of two evils. But if Omenuko had known that he would stay alive after the crime, he would not have sold those men. He was always depressed about what he had done and his conscience blamed him to no end. Even though he had fled from his town, that did not atone for his crime against the people and the land. In his mind, he was like a convicted murderer, a fugitive from justice.

CHAPTER FOUR
Omenụkọ's Life in Mgborogwu

The Chief of Mgborogwu welcomed Omenụkọ and his family and treated them with great affection. He held Omenụkọ in very high esteem and appointed him a councilor in his court. Omenụkọ was a man with many attributes: intelligence, resourcefulness, keen perception and wisdom; and because of these qualities he was further appointed a judge in Mgborogwu.

The Chief did many things to please Omenụkọ so that he would not regret his flight into Mgborogwu. He was never treated like a stranger. The chief gave a piece of land adjacent to his palace, to Omenụkọ and his brother Okorafo to build their houses, and assigned rooms to Nwabueze in the palace. He was a very famous and rich man, wealthy in cash and kind. He had barns of yams, cocoyams, and countless domestic animals. He lacked one thing though, and it caused him many sleepless nights. He had married many wives but none of them bore him children early enough. An old man, his oldest son was a mere teenager. Thus, he did not value very highly all the wealth he possessed because among his people, to be truly wealthy was to have money, be married, and have grown up sons who would inherit a man's property when he died. Such a man was referred to by his people as an "Ogaranya"—a man of means.

Years later, Chief Mgborogwu fell sick. It was a terrible illness. All kinds of *"dibia"* were called in to treat him: renowned *dibias*, diviners—big and small, and numerous healers all tried their hands to no avail. When things seemed eventually hopeless, Chief Mgborogwu called the elders and counselors in his court to make known to them his last wishes to be executed in the event of his death. He disclosed to them 'so and so; so and so. This is the way this goes and that is the way that goes.' He also implored them to make sure that his Warrant (staff of office) was not withdrawn when he died by the District Commissioner (DC), on the grounds that the heir-apparent, Obiefula, was not grown up enough to be chief. Furthermore, he indicated that it was his wish that Omenụkọ should hold the Warrant, acting as a regent, till Obiefula was of age. That was on the condition that the District Commissioner approved of it.

The people of Mgborogwu were very concerned by these declarations because they knew very well that an *Eze* does not say such things for nothing. They have a saying that if "an Ogaranya who has pronounced his last wishes fails to die, it is shame on death." In this case, however, Chief Mgborogwu died and Omenụkọ saw to it that he had a most befitting burial. He was accorded all the rites and fanfare which a great noble man who had mature sons received at death. Thus Chief Mgborogwu did not become a laughing stock to the world at his death. His people also had nothing to be ashamed of. Omenụkọ saw to all that and thus proved very useful to Chief Mgborogwu and his people at a most critical moment.

CHAPTER FIVE
The Last Wishes of *Eze* Mgborogwu

Omenụkọ was anxious to know how the people of Mgborogwu regarded their chief's last wishes. Therefore, he summoned them to a meeting and bought a few things with which to entertain them. They included palm wine, kola nuts, and a goat which he used in preparing food for them. Then he addressed them saying, "My brethren, 'it is always best to look for a black goat in the daytime; at night it is hard to tell apart a black goat and the night. You remember how our chief had said on his deathbed that he didn't want his Warrant chieftaincy to be withdrawn by the Whiteman on the grounds that Obiefula, his son, was not grown up yet to take his place as Chief. He did suggest that I, Omenụkọ, should hold his Warrant till Obiefula was of age. That was why I talked about looking for a black goat in the day time. I think that now is the proper time to approach the District Commissioner on the issue." Omenụkọ's speech was greeted with general approval. The people asked him a definite date when they could embark on his suggestion if they were all resolved to pursue it. Omenụkọ advised them that it would be best to pursue the matter right away. They all agreed to meet again in four days' time on their next market day to set a specific date for going to see the government officials. After they had dispersed, however, the people got together and held another meeting in secret from which Omenụkọ was excluded because they did not want him to know about it since the meeting was held to talk about him and his proposal.

The first question they asked themselves when they met was: "Do we really want Omenụkọ to hold this Warrant for Obiefula?" Secondly, they asked, "Who should live in the palace, Obiefula or Omenụkọ?" One man stood up and said, "if we allow Omenụkọ to act as regent till Obiefula is of age we should, therefore, let him live in the palace till he is no longer the Chief." Several others however objected to this suggestion. "What! That would never please any ear that hears it. Obiefula should live in the palace. It is true he is not the chief now but at least he should be able to detect when a roof is leaking and have it repaired. He would only approach Omenụkọ for difficult problems. If it is something that needs our action then Omenụkọ would inform us." This was applauded and adopted by the people, after which they dispersed to await the next meeting with Omenụkọ.

On the appointed day, all the people assembled at Chief Mgborogwu's palace. Omenụkọ remarked that a previous decision need not be rehearsed; it was confirmed merely by nodding. "Where do we stand now?" he asked. They stated that there was nothing else left to be done than to agree on the exact date to go to see the District Commissioner. As they were about to fix a date, one man declared that there was something he thought should be discussed before anything else, including the visit to the District Commissioner. They encouraged him to speak his mind. He then put the question to the audience: "Omenụkọ and Obiefula, who should live in the Palace?" When he sat down, a man called Uba stood up and replied:

"Omenụkọ should live in his own house near the court, while the heir-apparent, Obiefula, lives in the palace. Obiefula should right from now, be assigned some responsibilities so that he would begin to acquire some administrative skills and experiences. If we keep pampering him as a child, these things might be too difficult for him to handle when he comes of age. Let us assign to him domestic affairs in the court while Omenuko deals with the more complicated external matters." The people nodded in agreement and asked Omenuko what he thought of such an arrangement. He replied that it was all right with him. Obiefula equally acquiesced saying: "When my father said that water sustains the fish in the river, I heard it with my two ears. I would say in the same way that you the people sustain my strength." Everybody in the audience thanked Uba for his thoughtfulness, and then they took up the issue about the Warrant. They decided on meeting the District Commissioner on the Monday following their meeting. For the purpose of that trip, Omenuko purchased a ram, a cock, eggs, and groundnuts for presentation to the District Commissioner.

On the appointed day, they all including Obiefula, left for Awka, the government headquarters to see the District Commissioner. On arrival they met the Paymaster who told them that the District Commissioner was away on tour and was due back the following morning. When the Paymaster asked the purpose of their visit, they replied that the District Commissioner had told them to come after the burial of their Chief, to report to him, how things went.

"Fine," replied the Paymaster, "it will be proper for you to wait till tomorrow. He has to come back because the District Commissioner would be visiting here the day after tomorrow, and so the Assistant District Commissioner has to be here to receive him." They thanked him and then went back to where they were staying in town. While there, they conferred among themselves and decided that it would be much better to wait for two days and meet the Assistant District Commissioner and the District Commissioner together, so that both of them could give them the same reply at the same time. So when the Assistant District Commissioner came back the following morning, Omenuko and his group did not go to meet him.

The next day the District Commissioner arrived as was expected. The court clerk sent messages inviting all the court judges and chiefs to come and meet the District Commissioner on the second day of his arrival in Awka. Once more Omenuko and his delegation postponed their visit to the District Commissioner so that they could meet with him on the third day when all the court judges and big chiefs would be present as well.

When the chiefs arrived they were first met by the Assistant District Commissioner and later by all the government officials including the District Commissioner and the Paymaster. The chiefs greeted them "Morny Sir, Morny Sir." The District Commissioner took the register containing the names of all the big chiefs and court judges and called them by their names one by one. When he called Chief Mgborogwu, Omenuko whispered to Obiefula to answer. The Assistant District Commissioner informed the District Commissioner that the lad was the son of Chief Mgborogwu who died recently. After the roll call the District Commissioner told them what he had sent them for namely, to familiarize them with routine official procedures and operations.

When the District Commissioner finished his address to the chiefs, Omenuko told Obiefula to tell the District Commissioner that they had something they wished to discuss with him. When the District Commissioner asked him what the matter was, Obiefula told him that he and his people wanted to inform him that they had completed the burial of his father. "Furthermore," he added, "my father requested you to let Omenuko hold the Warrant for me until I am fully mature to assume the responsibilities." After he had said this, Omenuko promptly brought out the gifts and presented them to the Assistant District Commissioner. The Assistant District Commissioner showed them to the Paymaster and the District Commissioner. They were all happy and thanked Omenuko and his group. The District Commissioner then asked the members of the delegation: "Is it your wish that Omenuko should be given the Warrant for Mgborogwu until Obiefula comes of age?" They answered 'yes'. The District Commissioner did not turn down their request but he asked them to go home and come back on another appointed day for his formal decision. They went home rejoicing.

From that moment Omenuko began to attend the court once a week on a temporary basis until they could hear finally from the District Commissioner. Eventually the District Commissioner sent for them but Omenuko went only with Obiefula to see him. The District Commissioner said to Omenuko: "As from next month you will become a full and regular member of the Court as Chief of Mgborogwu. It will be your responsibility to appoint carriers and servants who would always bring me gifts of yams from you." "Leave that to me, I can do better than that even without being reminded," replied Omenuko delightfully. That was the end of the ceremony. The Paymaster, the Assistant District Commissioner and the District Commissioner all shook Omenuko's hands and from that moment Omenuko came to be addressed as "Chief." Omenuko in return, thanked the white men and greeted them "Morny Sir." He and Obiefula returned to Mgborogwu and Omenuko's term of office as Regent commenced.

CHAPTER SIX
The Reign of Omenụkọ as *Eze* Mgborogwu

The first court case which Chief Omenụkọ attended was one between a roadmaker and a court messenger. The two had fought and after the chiefs listened to their statements, they found both of them guilty and fined them one pound ten shillings each and warned them not to fight again. In the eyes of his colleagues, Omenụkọ was a very good and respectable chief. He had the interest of his people always at heart. The government officials also remarked his efficiency, his great sense of responsibility and his integrity as a ruler. Whenever he came to court, the other chiefs would not need anyone to remind them that this was a sensible man for it was perceived in everything he said and did. The questions he put to people in the witness box were very perceptive and constructive. At times when the chiefs as a body had an issue to take up with the District Commissioner or a request to make, it would be Omenụkọ who would invariably think of the best method of approach and he was always right. If you merely listened to his words, you would discern from them wit and wisdom. In effect, people would always go to him for advice and instructions. He was not only wise, he also had a generous and amiable disposition. He was a friend of the poor as well as the rich. He cared for and respected his neighbors and other people around him. Because of his humane acts and charming personality no one thought of him again as a stranger in Mgborogwu.

Nobody ever regarded or treated him as a stranger anymore because both he and his brothers had in addition married from Mgborogwu and the surrounding towns.

Omenụkọ and his brothers had become very prosperous and wealthy owning several barns of yams and countless domestic animals, including cows. There were people who would pawn themselves to Omenụkọ in order to get out of great financial troubles. This practice was not the same as slavery because the person only traded his services for a lump sum of money to solve some nagging problems. Thus, many people would approach Omenụkọ and say: "Our Master, please save me before my enemies finish me." "What do you want me to do for you?", Omenụkọ would ask. Then the man would prostrate on his knees and say, "My Master, my knees are on the ground. Please lend me such and such amount to pay off my debts. I shall come to live in your house, serve and work for you three days a week and do my own work on the fourth day (there being four working days in the week), to repay the money you lent me."

If the man is someone who Omenụkọ does not know very well, he would further try to find out how the man managed to get into debt. And after that he would try to find out something about his character asking such questions as: "Are you an honest man?" "Have you ever been caught stealing or accused of stealing?" "Do you bear false witness?" And to all these the man in need would reply: "I have never stolen from anybody and I have never given false witness." With that Omenụkọ would then give him the money he requested but the borrower must come to live in Omenụkọ's house to fulfill the other obligations he pledged.

In this way many borrowers came to live with Omenụkọ and his brothers working on Omenụkọ's farm lands. At this time Omenụkọ had become exceedingly rich, by far richer than when he was a merchant in his homeland. In his home town, he had three wives, his brother Okorafo had two, and Nwabueze had one. But now Omenụkọ's wives numbered seven, Okorafo's four, Nwabueze's two, while their youngest brother Ogbonnaya had one.

Whenever Omenuko thought about his past as against his present position and status, he thanked God on high and his brothers that he stayed alive. Only one thing still denied him peace of mind; that was the sale of his cousin Obioha together with other people's children into slavery. Unfortunately for him too, his two sisters who accompanied him in the flight, had died shortly afterwards.

As if those were not enough setbacks, the people of Mgborogwu conspired and held a secret meeting at this time, against Omenuko and his family. They believed that it was about time Omenuko gave back the Warrant to Obiefula who was then grown up enough to manage his own affairs. They decided on a date to go to communicate this demand to Omenuko. They swore that no one who attended the secret meeting should go back on their resolution. After the meeting, however, some members defected and went to Omenuko to reveal what they had discussed, so Omenuko knew in advance what day they would be coming to see him and why.

Before that date, Omenuko went to Awka and held talks with the District Commissioner. He told the District Commissioner that he was contemplating moving his residence to a distant forest area called Ikpa Oyi (waste land). When the District Commissioner asked him what would become of his people, those under him, Omenuko assured him that he would be moving along with them. Therefore, the District Commissioner consented to his plans. When he returned, he went and inspected the piece of land, Ikpa Oyi. He was not perturbed that the area was the notorious evil forest where dead criminals and people who died of abominable diseases were buried long ago. He had based all his future plans on that piece of land. The land, Ikpa Oyi, was so called because it was also a dumping ground for those who died especially of dreaded diseases such as swollen sickness, hernia, smallpox, as well as women who died in their pregnancies. It became a no-man's land, a vast expanse of land that everyone dreaded and no one dared step into for any reason.

Before long the people of Mgborogwu conspired again and held a meeting against Omenuko and his brothers. Again they swore that no one should go back on their resolution or betray their cause namely, forcing Omenụkọ to give back the Warrant to Obiefula. But as before, some of them still found their way back to Omenụkọ's residence and revealed to him without using actual words, what had been discussed at the meeting. They merely said to him: "spoken agreements are confirmed only with the nodding of the head." Thus they made sure that the oath of secrecy they took would not kill them. Omenụkọ was a very intelligent man, so he fully understood what they were alluding to.

On the appointed day, all the people assembled at Omenụkọ's house early in the morning. Omenụkọ welcomed them and they exchanged greetings. Omenụkọ asked one of his servants to bring a bowl of water and two kola nuts. He offered the kola nuts to his guests and then according to custom they said: "Chief, please break the kola." The Chief gave them one to break while he broke the other himself. The kola was given to Uba. First, with the clay chalk—nzu—he stenciled some lines on the ground before he uttered the incantations: "Earth come and chew kola, our ancestor Mgborogwu come and chew kola, God on high here's kola for you, kind spirits here's kola, whoever says I don't deserve what is mine, when he gets his, he won't be fit for it. I am for live-and-let-live, whoever objects to that let him be denied life. Let the kite perch and let the eagle perch too. Whichever obstructs the other, may his wings break!" And the people present affirmed with, "*I see!*—, so may it be!", to each of the prayers above. Next, Omenụkọ took the nzu and said his own prayer: "God on high come and chew kola, our ancestor Mgborogwu come and chew kola, may good prevail and evil not see the light of the day; good luck for me and my enemies, may the morning dew disperse all evil. Whoever wishes me death, may he be the first to die and go to bed before the chickens." Omenụkọ's people responded, "*I see!*, so be it!!"

Then the people said to him, "Chief, we have come to request you to consider giving back to Obiefula the Warrant of his late father, since he is now of age." "Fine", answered Omenụkọ, "but there is just one thing you people did which is very bad. I believe you held a secret meeting not once but twice in order to present this matter to me?" They all loudly denied, saying "Never!" We did no such thing." Omenuko continued however, "It is unpleasant to the ear, and something against the law, that a whole town should conspire and hold a secret meeting against just one individual. I can send all of you to prison for the offense." The people were frightened and begged him not to send them to prison. "Please our Master, do not send us to prison but rather tell us how best to go about this matter." Omenuko advised them that "the easiest way would be to go to the District Commissioner and present your case to him and tell him also that you conspired against me. The District Commissioner will tell you whether your action was right or wrong." They thanked him and requested some days to think the matter over and then they would come back to him to tell him their decision. And they all left. But shortly afterwards, they held another secret meeting without informing Omenuko. And when they assembled at his house again, they said to him: "Our Master, we have come to beg you to forgive us, and to say furthermore that whenever you yourself decide that Obiefula is mature enough to take over the chieftaincy, we would accept it as best for us." Omenuko then asked them, "Why didn't you say so the first time you came here?" They replied that they reached the decision at a later meeting and were asking for his forgiveness. Omenuko was very furious and burst out, "It was being said before that you held two secret meetings against me, and now you have held yet another one regardless of my previous warnings. You will all die in your folly. Can you at this stage convince the District Commissioner that you did not know that it was an offense for a whole community to conspire against one man? When I told you that you broke the law, if you didn't understand, didn't you also understand what I said you should do in effect?" Go home!," he ordered them. And they all left.

From that day onwards, Omenuko and his brothers intensified their private plans about leaving Mgborogwu. Where they were moving to was adjacent to the town but it could not be called Mgborogwu because you would have to cross another town before you reach Ikpa Oyi. Whatever happens the people of Mgborogwu could not take the trouble to walk the distance stretching over two towns in order to find fault with Omenụkọ.

Omenụkọ summoned the people of Mgborogwu and spoke to them in the following manner: "I do not want to live among you anymore. Since you my hosts have conspired and held secret meetings against my brothers and me, we have no confidence anymore in you. You never cared to remember again that it was I who redeemed your town and saved you from shame not long ago. You have forgotten everything and have chosen to treat me as your enemy. I will still regard you as my brethren; if you forget me, I shall not forget you so that the earth goddess may not kill me for my relationship with you all. By conspiring against me, you have removed me from among your group, isolating me like an outcast. For all these, I would now prefer to live apart from you like the stranger that you have made me. From today on, I shall be thinking about what you told me concerning the Warrant. I shall try to make up my mind whether it is worth seeing the District Commissioner or not." The people thanked him again and requested him to please "come up with pleasant and not bad decisions." Omenụkọ retorted: "The good decision you are asking for, could it be anything short of your desire that I hand back the Warrant to Obiefula? You can count on that as something already accomplished. Now, will you go home?" And they dispersed.

Shortly afterwards, Omenụkọ went again to see the District Commissioner. He said to him: "My people no longer want to change residence with me because the site I chose is the 'evil forest'. They have nevertheless told me that I still have to move because if I didn't they would in effect, have two chiefs in Mgborogwu! They have decided to appoint a chief to stay with those who would remain and they now look upon me as the chief of those who are moving with me to the new site." The District Commissioner and

Omenụkọ discussed the matter in very great detail and agreed that Obiefula would be accorded a separate Chieftaincy Warrant. It was not clearly stated by the District Commissioner whether it was supposed to be a new Warrant or that same one which he was to inherit from his father. Omenụkọ stressed to the District Commissioner that as soon as he was ready, he would leave for the new site and the District Commissioner urged Omenụkọ to keep him informed when the time came. After that, Omenụkọ and his brothers were hard at work preparing for their change of residence. When everything was ready except the completion of some houses, he requested the District Commissioner to excuse him from all official duties and functions till he had finished building his new houses, which would take about one or two months. "Two months should be sufficient but if you excuse me for three, that will be better." The District Commissioner granted his request and asked him to report for duty only when it was convenient for him to do so. Meanwhile Omenụkọ should have Obiefula deputize for him so that if the District Commissioner had any matter of real urgency requiring Omenụkọ's attention, he (the District Commissioner) would inform him through Obiefula. Omenụkọ was delighted and thanked the District Commissioner very much.

CHAPTER SEVEN
Omenuko and His Brothers Move into a New Location

Omenuko and all his brothers got ready to move to their new site along with all members of their households, including Omenuko's debtors. Because of their numbers, it became necessary for Omenuko to build several more houses at the new site to accommodate everybody. This entailed a lot of hard work. Omenuko appealed to the people of Mgborogwu for assistance, but they refused to help him. Omenuko, therefore, thought of a new strategy. He was no longer going to aim at solid and permanent houses. Rather he would aim at simple, small houses for a start and improve on them as time went on. When the buildings were completed, Omenuko again appealed to the people of Mgborogwu to help them move his property to the new residence, but again they declined. Omenuko was very surprised at them this time: "Oh! I thought you couldn't help us build the houses because I was building at the site of the evil forest, but now that I have finished building, what is so hard about helping us to move our things? Is this a worthy attitude in your sight?" But the people were not moved.

Omenuko and his brothers had to do everything by themselves. When they had moved all their things to the new site, Omenuko asked the Mgborogwu people if any of them would be interested in purchasing any of his old houses. Some of them who thought that

Omenụkọ had ill feelings towards them, said they wanted to buy the houses, even though they knew within themselves that they had no real intention of making him any offers. But there were some too, who still regarded Omenụkọ as a true friend, and these replied by saying that if the prices would not be too exorbitant, they would like to buy. Omenụkọ said to them "just make up your minds that you want to buy, I shall not fail to sell to you." One person spoke out that he was interested. He was followed by another but some others followed just for the fun of it. But from the offers the latter made, Omenụkọ was able to distinguish those who were serious from others who were merely faking and that helped him to determine who he could give the houses to and who not to. All those who showed real desire in the purchase, received the houses they wanted to buy free. In this way, Omenụkọ gave away all the houses belonging to him and his brothers.

Omenụkọ instructed Obiefula to prepare for a date in the future on which they would go to meet with the District Commissioner. Omenụkọ was at the same time preparing to receive people who wanted to "visit" his new home so he suggested to Obiefula that the visit to the District Commissioner would be best soon after his guests had come and gone. Three days after Omenụkọ had received all his guests, he sent for Obiefula and together they went to Awka to see the District Commissioner. The District Commissioner received them well and entered Obiefula's name on the list of Warrant chiefs. That notwithstanding, Omenụkọ urged Obiefula to ascertain from the District Commissioner whether it now meant that he (Obiefula) had become a full-fledged chief. "Yes, indeed.", replied the District Commissioner "You are a chief now. If I should need labourers or carriers or yams, it would be your duty to provide them. Furthermore, you must look after your people properly. It is no longer Omenụkọ's responsibility. When Omenụkọ was chief of Mgborogwu, there were no uprisings and no troubles. Omenụkọ is now chief only over those people living at the new site with him. Do you hear? You, yourself, are now the chief of those who are still living at the old site. Do you hear? If anything proves too difficult for you, you must not fail to consult Omenuko for advice. Do you hear?" To all these questions Obiefula replied, "Yes Sir" and the District Commissioner bade them farewell.

When they reached home there were celebrations and rejoicing everywhere in and around Mgborogwu. Omenuko's group was rejoicing and celebrating because their big man now had his own Warrant chieftaincy in their own autonomous community. He was no longer acting on behalf of anyone. On the other hand, Obiefula's group was also exceedingly filled with joy and was celebrating that at last their own Warrant had returned to the original family of Mgborogwu.

Omenuko thereafter invited all the other chiefs to come and visit his new home and see what it was that prevented him from attending court for three months. They all came and were full of praise for all his accomplishments. They gave him generous donations. Some gave him ten shillings and some five shillings, each according to his individual capacity. Omenuko thanked them and profusely entertained them with food and drinks. When they had all eaten and drunk to their fullest, he narrated to them what had transpired on his and Obiefula's visit to the District Commissioner, how the District Commissioner entered Obiefula's name on the list of chiefs, and gave Obiefula all the routine instructions that new chiefs were required to have. He further told them the special point made by the District Commissioner that if Obiefula failed in his duties to his people, it would not be Omenuko who would be blamed. Therefore, Obiefula was to render his services as faithfully as possible to his people, as they had been used to under the rule of Omenuko. That would be necessary especially as Omenuko would be concentrating on the interests of his own subjects at his new location far away from Mgborogwu.

When the chiefs heard all this, they rejoiced with Omenuko because they never really thought that it would have been wise to deprive Omenụkọ of a full chieftaincy of his own. At the end the visiting chiefs took leave of Omenụkọ and returned to their homes.

Omenụkọ now turned his attention to his brothers. They also had their share of the food and drinks. Afterwards, Omenụkọ spoke to them in these words: "My beloved, my being alive today was the work of God on high executed through all of you. Now listen. Okorafo, go to the court clerk and ask him to order for you the magic machine which talks with human voice in the white man's land'. Whatever it costs, I shall honor the bill. And you, Nwabueze, go to the shops at Onitsha and buy yourself a steel horse that the white man rides on from place to place. I will give you money to pay for it." It was the court clerk who told Nwabueze that the two items were called radio and bicycle. And finally to Ogbonna, Omenụkọ said, "Go and find yourself a beautiful girl from a good family, I shall be responsible for her bride price and other expenses." And then he added: "My beloved, there is only one thing that still makes me sleepless and restless whenever I recall it—those people who I sold into slavery long ago. No matter how much I try to brush it aside, it is quite impossible to forget." His brothers felt with him and told him that they would all have to pray for God's will in the matter. Omenụkọ was silent for a while and once again seemed lost in thought about the fate of those people he had sold long ago. It was clear to him that he would not be at peace with himself or with the world around him unless he made a full restitution for that abysmal crime.

CHAPTER EIGHT
Those Omenụkọ Sold into Slavery

Omenụkọ had a friend who was a trader from his original home town whose name was Igwe. He was a very good man, upright and respectable. Omenụkọ sent for him. Igwe was curious to know why Omenụkọ was sending for him, so he did not hesitate to answer his call as soon as the message reached him. Omenụkọ received him very well and entertained him on a grand scale. Late in the evening, they sat down to talk and Omenụkọ began the conversation with: "Igwe, my dear friend, I sent for you because I am in a serious difficulty, and it is causing me many sleepless nights. You are not a stranger in our land, therefore, you are aware of that thing I did which stands out as a very ugly and abominable act in the eyes of our people. I wish to know if I can find out through you the whereabouts of those people I sold and whether there is anything I can do to ransom them." The two men spoke to each other as frankly and exhaustively as possible. But first, they needed to establish a strong sense of mutual confidence between them. Therefore, they took an oath of secrecy and allegiance. Thereafter, Omenụkọ began with a proverb: "The hunter whose arrow hits the fast-fleeing deer gets rewarded with twenty arrows." Then he explained in plain words: "Anyone who comes out with a plan whereby I can even merely see those people that I sold, shall be rewarded with anything that person asks for." His friend encouraged him to be optimistic. "Fear not, God is alive—according to those who know the Holy Book."

They killed the goat with which they performed the oath of mutual trust. They ate some of it and saved some portions for their individual families. Igwe prepared to go but promised Omenụkọ that he would do his utmost and if he found anything worth reporting, he would not hesitate to inform Omenụkọ. Omenụkọ thanked him and Igwe left.

Incidentally, Igwe already knew the whereabouts of two of those people Omenụkọ sold. Omenụkọ's cousin, Obioha was living with Mazi Oji at 'Aru Ulo'. Another one was also living in 'Aru Ulo' but Igwe did not know in whose house he was living. Igwe tried to find out more but he could not on the particular trip he made after his visit to Omenụkọ. Shortly afterwards, Igwe went again to visit Omenụkọ and reported to him the progress he had made. He told Omenụkọ that he had found the whereabouts of two of the people. "Please what are their names?" Omenụkọ's anxiety was overpowering. Igwe replied: "Your cousin, Obioha is one of the two. He is living in the house of Mazi Oji. Elebeke Okoro is the other although I don't know exactly in whose house he is living." Omenụkọ spoke passionately to his friend: "My dear Igwe, my great desire now for which I made you the grand promise, is that you try and find out just where each one of them lives. I want to make you realize now that it was not an empty promise that I made you." And Omenụkọ went into his inner room and brought out some money which was tied in a small scarf. He counted out ten pounds and gave them to Igwe saying: "Each person found earns you five pounds. When you find where all the rest are, come and tell me and I shall pay you at this same rate." Omenụkọ next found out from Igwe when Bianko, Agbagwu and Oge Nta markets would be holding. After this, Igwe was ready to go. Omenụkọ advised him to be careful and observant. After Igwe had left, Omenụkọ called together his brothers and told them what happened and they were all very happy. He asked them if any of them would be willing to go to Mazi Oji to find out how much he would want as ransom for Obioha. Mazi Oji also would direct the person to wherever Elebeke Okoro was living so that his master would also name the fee for Elebeke's ransom. Nwabueze volunteered to go. Omenuko assigned a few other people to go with him and asked them to get ready in advance for the market day on which he would ask them to set off. Omenuko was calculating the market days on the basis of the information he got from Igwe. When the day on which he considered the roads to be least busy approached, he advised Nwabueze and his group to set off on their journey. But Igwe had forgotten to mention to Omenuko that the markets were no longer in Bende, instead they had been moved to Uzoakoli. Secondly, previously Bianko was the largest of the markets but now it was Agbagwu instead. Omenuko did not have these facts so that in his calculation, he had unknowingly mixed up the market days. Consequently, Nwabueze and his group ended up traveling when the traffic was heaviest. And when they asked those who were coming back from the market, which one they were returning from, they received answers quite opposite to what they had thought. They were all baffled by the inconsistencies. They rented a room at a place called 'Ugwu Aku' and while relaxing there, they were able to find out from the people around, the true nature of things and were able to get things straightened out. They stayed there for three days waiting for the traders to all pass on their homeward journey before they could continue their journey towards the market places. When the traffic was clear, they continued their journey. But when they reached Bende, Nwabueze was afraid he could not trust his sense of direction for the rest of the journey. He, therefore, hired some carriers from Bende who acted as escorts until they reached 'Aru Ulo' which was their final destination. He was able to get two carriers who led them to 'Aru Ulo'. Every Aru man no matter where he lives, must have a family which he calls his own at 'Aru Ulo'. So Nwabueze naturally wanted to go to his family in 'Aru Ulo' but then he remembered that act of Omenuko which was regarded as a crime even against kith and kin outside the homeland. He was therefore afraid to go to his Aru 'family'. Instead he decided in favor of the house of Mazi Oji as the place where they would stay. Obioha was not at home when they got to the house. He had gone to the market in 'Itu Agbanyim'. Nwabueze met Mazi Oji and introduced himself as Omenụkọ's younger brother. Mazi Oji was very excited and exclaimed. "Oh dear! Are you really his brother? How is he? How is my friend Omenụkọ? Is he alive?" And Nwabueze told him all about his brother Omenụkọ and explained that Omenụkọ had sent him specifically to Mazi Oji. "He asked me to find out from you whether you would be kind enough to let him ransom our cousin Obioha. And if you should agree to that, then you are to tell me how much you would want him to pay you." Those were Nwabueze's words. Mazi Oji exclaimed that Obioha was the head of all of his slaves and he was a man of a gentle disposition and trustworthy." "Fine," replied Nwabueze, "but I must add that it is not only Obioha that Omenụkọ wants to redeem, he also would like to know through you the whereabouts of the other young men he sold." Mazi Oji assured him that that would be simple. He pointed out that Elebeke was living in the house of Ezuma and that if pains were taken to look for the others, they would be found. "I hope you would kindly arrange to take me to Ezuma's house so that I can make the same request to him for the liberation of Elebeke," implored Nwabueze. Later they agreed to go to Ezuma's house the following day. But without Nwabueze knowing it, Mazi Oji went and met Ezuma the same evening to confer with him on whether or not they should accede to Omenụkọ's request. Without hesitation, Ezuma answered, "We have no choice but to accede to Omenụkọ's request. These young men are also our children. We all belong to Aru whether we live at home or outside. If Omenụkọ treats us well, we simply have to cooperate with him. Remember, too these are the days of the white man. If these young men express a desire at some point to be returned to their homes, we would have to let them go, that is, if we refuse to liberate them now. If care is not taken, we might even be in trouble then and they could still go home as they wish, without our having to be paid any money for that." Mazi Oji saw that Ezuma's words were true, so he asked Ezuma how much he thought they should ask from Omenụkọ. His friend suggested that they wait and hear what offer Omenụkọ makes then know how to react. They left the matter at that pending the meeting with Nwabueze in the morning.

At their meeting the next morning, after they had greeted each other by their praise names and eaten kola, Nwabueze put before them the object of his mission. Mazi Oji and Ezuma excused themselves and went outside the house to confer. But they came back soon afterwards and suggested that the discussions be postponed till the next day to see if Obioha who went to a distant market could be back and participate in the discussions. Nwabueze agreed to that and they adjourned.

Obioha, however, came back from the market that same night. When he saw his cousin Nwabueze, he was very delighted and received him very well as if there was no grudge or ill feeling between them. When the two were conversing alone, Nwabueze told Obioha the purpose of his visit. Obioha was exceedingly pleased when he heard those words. "Even if you do not succeed," he said with tears in his eyes "I am happy at the initiative".

He then told Nwabueze about some of the other people that Omenụkọ sold too. Oti, had died the previous year and although Arisa was still alive he had emaciated beyond recognition from a terrible ailment. "Where does he live?" asked Nwabueze. "Here, he too lives in this town in an area called Obinkita". At this point, Mazi Oji sent for Obioha and told him the reason for his cousin's visit. Obioha diplomatically replied that that was a matter between his master Oji and Nwabueze. "If it suits you, it suits me fine too," he added. In the morning all the parties again assembled at Mazi Oji's house and continued the talks. After a short while, Mazi Oji, Ezuma, Obioha and Elebeke went outside to confer among themselves. While there, Ezuma talked to them in a proverb saying 'Before the plaintiff begins to rejoice about the evidence in his favor, he should make sure that the defendant has pleaded guilty." He indirectly alluded that Obioha and Elebeke should first decide if they wanted to be ransomed. Both of them replied that it was for their masters to say whether they were in favor of Omenụkọ's request or not. Mazi Oji assured them that if their own relation made the move to redeem them, that was a good gesture. "Aru Elugwu and Aru Ulo are both the same. Therefore, we would accede to his request." Then they all went back and informed Nwabueze that they would agree to his demands, and furthermore, they would help him to locate Arisa. Nwabueze was very pleased and thanked them profusely. They adjourned the talks at that point. And Nwabueze retired to Obioha's house for the night. The following day, Nwabueze approached Mazi Oji and Ezuma and requested them to name the fee which Omenụkọ would have to pay them. They conferred among themselves alone and then came back and told him to ask Omenụkọ to remember that the people concerned were as much his relatives as theirs so he could simply refund their original payment. Nwabueze then went back to Obioha's house, quite pleased because he was making real progress in his mission. The following day Nwabueze left for home to give Omenụkọ an account of his progress so far. Omenụkọ was filled with joy and happiness and thanked Nwabueze very much. He wanted to act immediately on Nwabueze's agreement with Mazi Oji and Ezuma and, therefore, wanted him to go back immediately to implement the decisions reached. Unfortunately, Nwabueze was bitten by a snake that night and the pain was increasing every moment such that he could not undertake the journey again. Omenụkọ appealed to his other brother Okorafo saying: "Please, I do not want to lose anytime at all. I request you to go immediately to 'Aru Ulo' with Nwabueze's escorts. When you get there you should pay Mazi Oji forty pounds, and pay the same amount to Ezuma. You should also contact the man in whose house Arisa is living and pay him forty pounds too. You are not a small child, therefore, you must explore every possibility to locate the other young men too." Okorafo and

Nwabueze's escorts then left for Aru Ulo. Meanwhile Ọmenụkọ sent for a medicine man to treat Nwabueze's snake bite.

When Okorafo and his men reached Ozuitem, they were arrested by the town guards for violating their night curfew as they were trying to cross the town at night. The night curfew was in keeping with an initiation ceremony that was going on. Okorafo told the guards that he himself had been initiated so they tested him on the "password" of the in-group. "Come then and show us the head of the rope", they told him. And he gave the correct answer. He was released but his four companions had not been initiated ever before so the guards fined them five shillings each and allowed them to continue on their journey. When they reached Mazi Oji's house, he immediately recognized Okorafo and called him by name. Later Obioha took Okorafo to his house to pass the night.

In the morning Okorafo told Mazi Oji that he had come in connection with the negotiation which Nwabueze had begun with him. Mazi Oji then sent for Ezuma for he felt that nothing should be discussed in his absence. When Ezuma arrived, he went out with Mazi Oji to confer and later Mazi Oji told Okorafo to repeat to everyone's hearing what he said to him previously. Okorafo said, "Please my brethren, I was sent by Ọmenụkọ to come and continue with you the negotiation which Nwabueze had started about Obioha, Elebeke and Arisa." They replied that they still stood on their statements to Nwabueze, adding: "These young men are yours as well as ours, so if they agree to go back with you, we have no objection, provided we are refunded what we paid for them." Okorafo again thanked them for their cooperation. He brought out his bag, counted out and paid forty pounds for each of the two men. They thanked him very much in return. Obioha and Elebeke stood up and bowed to Mazi Oji and Mazi Ezuma, and also thanked and shook hands repeatedly with Okorafo. At the end, Okorafo asked the men about Arisa. "That is not a difficult problem," replied Mazi Oji and Mazi Ezuma simultaneously. Mazi Ezuma added: "I'll send someone right away to tell him that you are here and you desire to see him." Elebeke was sent to go and call Arisa and when he came back, he assured them that Arisa would come as soon as he finished the palm wine tapping he was doing at that time.

When Arisa saw Okorafo, he started to shed tears, but Okorafo begged him to stop. Arisa asked Okorafo about the condition of numerous people he had known at his master Omenụkọ's house. Okorafo assured him that everyone was alive except the two sisters who had died soon after their flight. Arisa expressed his deep sympathy for the death of Omenụkọ's sisters—Nwanu and Udeola. Then Okorafo informed him that the purpose of his visit was to take him back home with them. "Are you willing to return with me to our home town?" Before he could reply, Arisa wanted to know first, the reactions of Obioha and Elebeke to the offer. Okorafo did not answer that but rather passed on the question to Obioha and Elebeke themselves. "Accept the offer, Arisa because we both have accepted it. Okorafo will see to the other details with your master as he has done with our two masters." Arisa was happy with their advice but he refused to commit himself until Okorafo had talked with his master. "As soon as that is done," he said, "I will be ready to leave with you anytime you choose. "Okorafo was very pleased and promised Arisa that they would come to see his master the next day but that they would send someone right away to inform his master that some visitors would be knocking at his door in the morning. Arisa then went home to get ready some refreshments he would serve Okorafo and his group when they visit the next morning. A messenger was dispatched too as Okorafo promised, to Arisa's master, Okpara. Okpara was told to stay at home the following day because Mazi Ezuma would be bringing him a special guest. "That's fine," mused Okpara, "a man sitting in the comfort of his home, never develops cramps from waiting for a guest." He called Arisa and asked him to reserve for him, whatever palm wine he tapped the next morning. Arisa was getting only two jars of wine every morning, so he promised to give one to his master and reserve the other for himself for the same occasion. In the morning, Okpara's visitors arrived, including Mazi Oji, Mazi Ezuma, Obioha, Elebeke and Okorafo and his group. After they had eaten kolanut, Okorafo urged Mazi Oji to open the discussion. Mazi Oji responded with a proverb which states that "only relatives of a dead person know which end of the coffin his head is placed". He then added that saying the opening words belonged to Okorafo. Okorafo then addressed Okpara saying: "Please my father; it is to your house that I have come to request you as well as Mazi Oji and Mazi Ezuma, on behalf of my brother Omenụkọ, to permit us to redeem our brethren—Obioha, Elebeke, and Arisa. These two chiefs have already negotiated with me concerning Obioha and Elebeke, so my plea is now to you, Mazi Okpara." Okpara then requested to confer with the two chiefs alone for a short while. At their private audience, Mazi Oji and Mazi Ezuma told Okpara that they had already taken back their ransom money. "How much then should I ask him to pay me as well?" Okpara wanted to know. The two men advised him simply to tell Okorafo that he had no objection to his plan. When they got back, they told Okorafo that Okpara had no objection to his request but however since "you have 'seen' us, what remains is for you to 'see' Okpara. As the saying goes, if you treat a child the way you treated his playmates, he would be satisfied." Okorafo replied that that would not constitute a problem for him. They postponed further discussions till the next day asserting that something must be wrong if a palm tree bears fruit the very day it sprouts! Thereafter, Okpara presented them the jar of palm wine he had reserved for them, but no sooner had he presented it than Arisa came out with another jar which he gave to Okpara to "please offer this kola to our visitors." While they were drinking, Arisa was overheard in private protesting to his master: "Why couldn't you at least ask my opinion in the matter?" His master apologized saying: "You are right, but I did not seek your opinion because Mazi Oji and Mazi Ezuma and your two friends had already agreed and so all I did was to go along with them. Furthermore, it was so that I could get a chance to consult you that we postponed further talks till tomorrow." Arisa was satisfied with the explanation and the matter was dropped. When they finished drinking, the visitors left.

On their way home, Okorafo asked Mazi Oji if he thought that Arisa was not justified in making that protest to his master. "I think, Okpara's behavior in not seeking his opinion was bad," Mazi Oji answered, and then explained that Okpara must have acted the way he did because, "as you might know, Arisa was not bought with his (Okpara's) own money. Arisa was like any other thing that he inherited from his late father." Elaborating, Okorafo added: "This sort of thing happens also even with wives; if one's wife is chosen for him by his parents and it happens that later in life the young man fights with his wife, he would state that if he had chosen a wife by himself, the last mistake he would make would be to marry this type of wife his parents chose for him. But in a situation where a man had the option to choose his wife, he would have no one to blame for whatever the girl he chose turned into later on. I believe that any sum of money I pay Okpara as ransom for Arisa, I shall be justified and he should receive it with gratitude. He invested nothing on Arisa." Mazi Oji entirely agreed with Okorafo. When they reached home, Okorafo asked Obioha and Elebeke for suggestions on the possible day for their departure for home. Elebeke assured him that they were at his pleasure and command, having just been liberated by him. They, therefore, would accept whatever time he judged best for them to begin their journey. Okorafo told them that they would leave the day after tomorrow, to which both men agreed.

The next day, they went back to Okpara's house. After they had been served kola and drinks, Okorafo implored them to hasten matters for his sake, but was reminded by Okpara that everything that remained to be done depended on him (Okorafo) because both he (Okpara) and his servant Arisa had no objections to Okorafo's proposals. "In that case then, what comes next?" asked Okorafo. "I thought I already told you to treat a child like you treated his mates and he would be happy," answered Okpara. Then Okorafo counted thirty pounds and gave it to Okpara saying, "Take this, you realize that Arisa belongs to all of us." Mazi Oji interjected that that was the basic consideration he had for the part he played in the whole affair. Okpara thanked Mazi Oji, and also Okorafo as he accepted the money. He then wanted to know what time Okorafo and the young men intended to set off. Okorafo told him that they planned to do so early the next day.

"Did you hear that?" Okpara asked Arisa, who answered with: "My ears are open." Okorafo drew Arisa aside and told him to get ready as early as possible. "Don't worry about your possessions. Leave everything for your master and avoid any conflict with him." Okorafo assured him that Omenuko had made adequate provisions for the rehabilitation of the three of them just liberated. Arisa agreed to be ready on time. Thus the negotiations were brought to an end. Okorafo thanked Okpara for his cooperation.

They returned to Mazi Oji's house and when they had rested sufficiently, Obioha suggested to Okorafo to inform the other members of their host families that they would be departing the next day. He urged Okorafo to stress that they were going away by the mutual agreement of both sides. Some of the people, when told, wept and said they would miss the liberated men dearly. Some took it bravely and in good spirit, pointing out that it was delightful that the whole arrangement proceeded peacefully. "To be otherwise would have seemed like a battle between two brothers, since Aru Ulo and Aru Elugwu were after all, of the same stock." The following morning Okorafo sent one of his companions with Obioha to go and fetch the others. First they went for Elebeke. When he was about to leave with the group, his master Ezuma gave him one pound and ten shillings to buy gifts and souvenirs for members of his family at home. Elebeke knelt down and thanked him very much. Then they went for Obioha. There again, his master Mazi Oji, gave him two pounds and ten heads of tobacco, as presents for his people at home. Obioha felt flattered. He bowed and thanked his master profusely.

Okorafo remarked to Mazi Oji that he was not really expecting "these things" from them. "Arisa arrived just now and showed me one pound which his master Okpara gave him. Elebeke equally showed me his own one pound ten shillings, and now you have presented two pounds to Obioha. Well, thank you. May God and our ancestors reward you all abundantly."

The preparations for the journey dragged on until late in the evening. When they were at last quite set to leave, the four of them went and bid Mazi Oji good-bye. Obioha took Elebeke with him to go and bid Mazi Oji's wife good-bye. When she saw them, she burst into tears. Obioha too, wept. Elebeke had to play the role of comforting both and urging them to stop crying. He reminded them that Obioha was not going away to die and there were possibilities of occasional visits. The elderly woman lamented: "Oh! My son Obioha, so it is indeed true!" She sighed deeply and accepted the fact that it was not parting forever. She drew Obioha to herself and embraced him saying, "Indeed one is like his name, OBIOHA (endeared to all) my child, go in peace!" Obioha had lived true to his name.

That same night they set off on their journey home. It was a very peaceful and pleasant trip and there were no incidents of any type anywhere on their way. When Omenuko saw Obioha, Elebeke and Arisa, he was very, very happy and rejoiced as he welcomed them home. When he had fully welcomed them, he asked them to relax and make themselves at home. Then he called three of his wives and gave them a goat each saying: "Use each goat for the meal of each of these returned men." He also gave them five shillings each to buy fish for the same meal and urged them to make the food delicious indeed. He called in Obioha and assured him that his mother was still alive and he informed the other two about the conditions of their families. Elebeke's parents were both still alive and Arisa's people were all well. Despite their natural urge to be among their families without delay, Omenuko restrained them and urged them to stay with him for a month. Each of the three wives, he had earlier appointed to cook food, was to continue for the whole month, looking after the person she prepared that first meal for. Omenụkọ encouraged the three men to feel free to ask for whatever they had taste for without regard to cost. They were full of thanks for all his concern and generosity for them after so many years. They felt flattered by every effort he made to make up for the ugly past. So they said to him: "We knew very well that you had no ill feelings towards us, therefore, whatever happened, we were sure that you could never feel at ease as long as we were in bondage. We knew moreover that you would never have dreamed of that act if it were not for that tragic event on that fateful day. We believed, therefore, that you acted out of the shock and impulse of the moment. We never cursed you for a day, rather we wished you well all along." Obioha who was Omenụkọ's own cousin added: "If we had dared to curse you, if the curse of the others failed, mine would not, realizing that I would have invoked our blood relationship in any pronouncement I made against you." Omenụkọ expressed how happy he was at the thought that they did realize that he was terribly upset when he did what he did, and not necessarily that he had anything personal against any one of them. "More than anything else," he said, "I am very happy that you are here today and we are talking face to face!" He asked them to relax and try and let bygones be bygones. He was determined to make up fully for every error of the past.

It was not until a day later that Okorafo was able to narrate to Omenụkọ everything that took place in their journey to and from Aru Ulo. He told him about Mazi Oji's hospitality and cooperation all the time, and also how much he paid as ransom to each of Obioha's, Elebeke's, and Arisa's masters. He also told Omenụkọ about their arrest at Ozuitem and how he secured the release of his companions upon payment of fines. Omenụkọ was delighted at every stage of the story and when Okorafo finished, Omenụkọ praised him very highly calling him "Ome kam" ("He who does like I do"). He confirmed that Okorafo acted in each of the circumstances, exactly as he, Omenụkọ, would have done.

After all this, Omenụkọ sent for the families of Elebeke and Arisa. When they arrived and saw the relations they had never thought they would set eyes on again, they exclaimed: "Who are these? Are they real?" Omenụkọ told them that he had invited them to come and join him in "seeing and making sure that they are indeed real." The visitors were overwhelmed and did not know what to expect next. But after Omenụkọ had entertained them, he explained to them that they would have to go back the next day but he would prefer to keep the returnees for a month. Then he told Elebeke's parents to "go and find for Elebeke two beautiful girls for marriage." When they had concluded all the negotiations, they should ask him for the money. And he charged Arisa's people to do the same thing for Arisa. The two families thanked him for all his kindness and generosity. They passed the night and returned home the following day.

When the two families initially received Omenụkọ's invitation, they were not scared to go to his house. This was because Omenụkọ's friend Igwe, had already given them hints from the day he knew of Omenụkọ's plans. So when they received the invitation, they believed that it was for something good and they were proved right by what they saw and by how Omenụkọ received them. When they reached home, it was no problem at all finding wives for Arisa and Elebeke as was directed by Omenụkọ. And when they had concluded the negotiations, Omenụkọ gave them all the money needed as he had promised.

At the end of one month when Elebeke and Arisa got ready to go home, Omenụkọ gave each of them seven pounds in cash and various other gifts. But before they left, he sent for their families again and entertained them as before, all of them eating together this time with Omenụkọ's family to show, according to custom, that harmony and peace had been restored. Omenụkọ specially wanted an assurance from the families of the young men that none of them had any further grudges or ill will towards him. They fully reassured him concluding with: "May life go well for you and for us too; may we all be safe in whatever we do. May God and our ancestors bless our reunion!" Omenuko then handed the two men back to their families, and requested them to visit him from time to time to tell him how they were doing. Each one of them thanked Omenuko again and again before they finally left. But shortly after they had left, Omenuko recalled them and requested that they play down the celebration of their happy reunion. He pleaded: "You know that I did not succeed in bringing back everybody; if you celebrate too profusely or loudly, it would make the families of the two boys I couldn't find very sad and ill-disposed towards me. I need time to see how to make amends to them." The two families promised him that they would not do anything that would upset the unlucky families. He thanked them again and then they finally left.

A long time after these events, Omenuko's youngest brother, Ogbonna, one day took Obioha with him to visit his in-laws. On their way back, Obioha confided in Ogbonna saying: "I wonder why 'our father' was able to do so much for Elebeke and Arisa and nothing for me at all!" Ogbonna assured him that Omenuko certainly must be thinking about him, for he was not the type of person who would have to be reminded before he could do good for others. Ogbonna took to heart those words, but one day he couldn't resist mentioning the matter to Okorafo, who directly told Omenuko about it. Consequently, Omenuko spoke to Obioha explaining the whole situation to him: "My child, of course I have you in mind always and do care for your welfare. There is just one thing you haven't been told. At first when we fled from home, we took refuge at the court of Chief Mgborogwu. When he died, I was appointed chief in his place. But after sometime his people started being mean and vicious towards me. I was forced to leave that place. In effect, I am not now a citizen of Mgborogwu and I have for long been rejected by my original homeland. The primary thing I should do now, is to seek a reconciliation with our townspeople, and appease the gods and ancestors that I had greatly offended and sinned against, and thus re-establish myself in their good judgments. After that, anyone from our family who needs to marry, can then go boldly into our town and make his or her choice. When I have settled with our people, I shall certainly take up the issue of your marriage and welfare." Obioha was satisfied with his uncle's explanations and accepted them with joy.

CHAPTER NINE
Omenụkọ Is Homesick

Omenụkọ began thinking very seriously about his reunion with his townspeople and how to approach it to ensure a smooth success. He felt that it would not be proper to seek outside mediation because he was not quarrelling with his people. He knew that he was at fault. He had done something to them which was mean and horrible. Therefore, he had to find a way to win their acceptance and reintegration.

Omenụkọ decided again to ask for the assistance of his friend Igwe since Igwe did not fail him in their first deal and encounter. So he sent for Igwe, who came as soon as he got the message. When Igwe was within range of hearing, Omenụkọ shouted his praise name: "The One Who Recovers What Is Lost!" and Igwe responded with his friend's own praise name: "One Who Fulfils his Promise!" They laughed and joked and felt at ease with each other. Omenụkọ served Igwe kolanut and afterwards he began to unfold to him the throbbing of his mind. "My dear friend, it is only a beast in the forest that goes to a tree trunk to relieve an itch; a man usually goes to a fellow man. I once appealed to you and you answered me and fought like a man. Please take a handshake for that" (and Igwe did). "Now listen again. I sinned against gods and people in our land a long time ago. My actions were dictated by circumstances beyond my control. Now I am anxious to make peace with the gods and my people alike. My dear friend, I am as confused as an adult who resorts to sucking his mother's breasts!" His friend assured him that there must be a way out of every human dilemma no matter how complex. "You have not forgotten, have you, that we have priests in our land? Aniche, the priest for Earth goddess and Iyiukwa, the chief priest of the Skygod are the two who can bring peace and harmony between a man and his fellow men as well as a man and the gods."

Omenụkọ begged Igwe to please find out for him what it would take to effect reconciliation between him and his people as well as appease the gods. He gave Igwe money with which to buy the palm wine that would be required by the priests before they could outline the things that Omenụkọ would need to do.

Igwe first went to Aniche, the priest of the Earth goddess. When they had drunk the wine that Igwe brought, Igwe explained the purpose of his visit. The priest could not restrain himself. He exclaimed: "It won't be my ears alone that would hear this—you have to go and come again sometime so that I can call together our people to come and hear *this*!" He later told Igwe that he could come the next day, and so Igwe went home. In the morning Igwe went back carrying another jar of palm wine. When he reached the priest's house, the people had not yet come but it didn't take time before they all arrived. Igwe presented the wine and repeated what he had told the priest the previous day.

"Yes," admitted Aniche, "That was what he told me yesterday and I thought I had better call all of you to come and hear it. Now that you are all here, speak your minds because it is not an occasion for going to confer secretly before voicing an opinion." They urged the priest to speak on their behalf and they would accept his position. Looking Igwe straight in the eye, the priest said: "Tell Omenụkọ he would have to bring a bull, eight eggs, one cock, eight big yams and eight small yams. When he has brought these things, he would have fulfilled his obligations and the land would be cleansed to appease the goddess. He will stand right again in the eyes of the people and the gods, provided he also goes to ascertain, and fulfill the wishes of the Skygod." Igwe assured him that Omenuko had equally delegated him to ascertain the wishes of the Skygod through his chief priest Iyiukwa. Igwe then rose and went home.

The following day, he took palm wine to the chief priest of the Skygod and presented Omenuko's case to him also. It sounded incredible to Iyiukwa and he advised Igwe to go home! Ridiculing Igwe further, he asked, "Go and ask Omenuko, the sheep that wants to grow horns, how strong is his neck?" "What does that mean?" asked Igwe, puzzled. Iyiukwa answered amidst a mirthless laughter: "Your Omenuko who wants to make peace with angered deities, can he go through the rituals doing everything that would be asked of him?" Igwe assured him that Omenuko would be willing to do everything required and wishes to know what they are. "Now please list them to my hearing," Igwe pleaded. "Alright, a mother sheep, a hen (old layer), a big cock, eight eggs, a piece of george cloth, a basket of yams, a basket of cocoyams, a kolanut pod, one alligator pepper, four kolanuts, eight lumps of nzu, a jar of palm wine that never touched the ground, and another ordinary jar of palm wine. If Omenuko can bring all these, the ritual shall be performed for him and it shall be well with him." Igwe thanked him and left.

But sometime later, Iyiukwa realized that he had missed one important item on the list. So he sent again for Igwe. When Igwe arrived, he told him that an important item had been left out on the list he had earlier prescribed for Omenuko. "Omenuko should not fail to bring four bright feathers plucked from the wings of an eagle."

Igwe had then the complete list of requirements, so he left and later on went to report the outcome of his inquiries to Omenuko. Omenuko listened with joy and eagerness to his account. At the end, he told Igwe that it appeared that any further action would be dependent on when all the listed items had been procured. "In that case, "he added, "we will talk again as soon as I have procured them." Igwe agreed with him and then turned to go. Omenụkọ looked at his friend and said, "I hope you wouldn't mind, if I took up your interests last." "Not at all," Igwe assured him. "Don't worry about me yet. Let's find what we are looking for first." On that note they mutually agreed to finish the big task first before sitting down to enjoy.

CHAPTER TEN
Omenụkọ Reconciles with His Home People

Omenụkọ bought all the things that the priests outlined for him except the feathers of an eagle. This was because he had two eagles which he had been rearing in his house. When he had bought all the other things, he sent for Igwe. When his friend arrived, Omenụkọ told him that all listed items had been bought. So Igwe went back home, eager to find out from the priests the next step to be taken. When the priests heard this, they told Igwe to ask Omenụkọ to come down with those things himself because the ritual was not something that someone else could deputize for him. As part of the ritual, he would have to touch with his lips some of the eggs and then throw them away. Some of the people around would also have to do the same thing. Then they explained more clearly to Igwe saying: "The whole thing is what is called 'oriko', communal ritual meal shared with gods and ancestors. Everything will be killed and cooked and then everybody will take a piece and eat and at the same time portions would be offered to our gods and ancestors." Igwe promised to convey all they said to his friend so that Omenụkọ could fix the date when he would come. But Igwe did not go to Omenụkọ by himself, rather he sent one of the young men in his house to convey the message to Omenụkọ. When Omenụkọ heard everything, he selected two men from his house together with Igwe's messenger to take the bull down to Igwe's house so that Igwe would look after it till he (Omenụkọ) arrives in four days' time. He asked them also to tell Igwe to inform the priests the day that he would arrive. When they had left, Omenụkọ called his brothers together to suggest who among them should accompany him on the appointed day. They decided that only Nwabueze should accompany him.

On that day Omenụkọ gathered all the other items he had bought and took also a whole eagle instead of the four feathers asked for. When he reached the town, he went straight to Igwe's house. It was already dark when he arrived but they sent a message to the two priests that he had arrived and would be seeing them the next day. The priests told him they would be waiting as the saying goes, "a man never gets tired waiting in his own house." Then Omenụkọ asked Igwe what they should do about wine, something Omenụkọ had forgotten to tell the people who brought down the bull to remind Igwe to place orders for. But his friend Igwe did not forget. He assured Omenụkọ that they would get all the wine they needed but special arrangements would have to be made for the 'palm wine that never touched the ground'. Igwe then went and made the arrangements accordingly. Omenụkọ and Igwe did not sleep that night till daybreak. They were busy chatting and filling each other in on the events of the past years. Nwabueze, Arisa and Elebeke stayed up late also talking and catching up with recent events.

In the morning Igwe sent some people to go and buy all the other wine needed. When they came back, Igwe then sent word to the priests that they were on their way. They went first to Aniche who promptly sent a messenger to go and call "the people of the land." When they had all gathered, no kolanut was presented to Omenụkọ because the ritual had not yet been performed and no one could share anything with him including kolanut. They asked him to do what he had come to do. He brought out the bull, the eight eggs, the white cock, the eight big yams, and the eight small yams and told Igwe that he was presenting this "to the people of the land" so that he can re-establish common ties with them for peace and harmony. Omenuko further added, now addressing the people: "Please, whoever meets or sees me anywhere, should henceforth regard me as one of you. You are my people and I am one of you. From today onwards, I would be ready to make up for any misdeeds of the past and would welcome suggestions from individuals on how I would go about this. Let me point out that there are no laws of our land that I forgot while in my place of exile. Although I was in another people's land (as their chief), I was still observing the laws and customs of my homeland." At this point Igwe stood up and thanked his friend, then pointing at the things Omenuko brought, he said to the chief priest: "These are the things Omenuko was required to bring for the ceremony. And we have heard with our own ears all of Omenuko's declarations. These things are now in your hands." The people thanked both Omenuko and Igwe. They selected a few young men to kill the cow and the cock. The head of the cow and the head of the cock were cooked in one pot for the elders. In a separate pot four eggs, and the eight yams were cooked. When everything was cooked thoroughly, they were emptied in one large open wooden platter. Then the meat from the cow was cut into small pieces and so was the chicken. These were to be offered in part to the gods when libation was to be poured by the chief priest. After these things, the chief priest took the four uncooked eggs and placed them in front of the people. Then he proceeded to perform the ceremony. He rubbed his mouth four times with the eggs saying: "Whatever I said about Omenuko, evil or bad, or against him and his brothers, is hereby wiped off today. We are all one people with them again. Our fathers, please hearken. The voice of the people is the voice of our gods. We are all one now. Whatever we abhor or look upon as taboo, they abhor too. Whatever we eat as food is eaten by them too. Whatever preserves our life, may it preserve theirs too. Whatever removes our life removes theirs now, too." After the chief priest, each person stood up, took one egg and did what the chief priest had just done and repeated the same words he had spoken. One by one, they all did this. Omenụkọ too, did like them. When all that was over, they sent one man to go and throw the eggs into the evil forest. After the man had done so, they began to eat the things cooked. They shared out the meat in portions and each person took his due share. While they were still drinking Omenụkọ said to them: "Please my brethren, I cannot stay till we finish all the wine, because I have to see the chief priest Iyiukwa also tonight." They permitted him to leave and Igwe accompanied him. When they got to the priest's house, they brought out everything they had been directed to buy: the sheep, the hen, the cock, the eight eggs, the george cloth, the yams, coco yams, kolanuts, alligator pepper, eighty pieces of nzu, the wine that never touched the ground, the other palm wine, and the eagle. As before, Omenụkọ requested Igwe to present those things on his behalf to Iyiukwa adding that his only prayer was that the gods might be appeased so that they might again be favorably disposed towards him. What he was asking of Iyiukwa was to restore for him, an affinity with the deities. Igwe presented the things to Iyiukwa and urged Iyiukwa to note in particular that instead of the feathers that he was asked to bring, Omenụkọ had brought a whole live eagle. That at least was enough to prove Omenụkọ's seriousness and genuine longing for all forms of reconciliation. The chief priest rose and shook the hands of both men saying: "You two are tough and great." Then he went into his inner room and brought out a small bell with which he summoned the vultures. He went outside and said, "This is the time I shall find out if the deities are happy" (with Omenụkọ). He began to jingle the small bell and it sounded: "tinom! tinom! tinom! tinom! tinom! tinom! tinom! tinom!" The vultures flew down from all angles! Iyiukwa ran back and quickly killed one of the fowls, sliced it into very small pieces and threw the pieces to the vultures. They picked and ate them up. He then ran back into the house and said excitedly to Omenụkọ, "Shake my hand, everything will be well!" The response of the vultures was an affirmation that the gods and ancestors had accepted Omenụkọ's peace offering. At the end of all this, Iyiukwa took one of the fowls and killed it. He also killed the sheep and set them boiling in the same pot. He put in the same pot also the yams which he had peeled and sliced, and also the four eggs. As these were cooking, he took out the remaining four eggs, one kola nut, four whorls of alligator pepper, which he had shredded, forty pieces of nzu, and the palm wine that never touched the ground stored in a bottle. He assembled all these together and proceeded to "wipe" his mouth with the eggs. And as he did this, he said, "May the mouth that spoke evil begin from today to speak well of Omenŭkọ; the voice of the people is the voice of our ancestors and the deities." He took the kolanut and did likewise with it. He did the same thing again with the nzu, and finally washed his mouth with the wine in the bottle, spitting it out seven times. Then he asked Omenŭkọ to repeat everything he had done. Thereafter, he gathered all the materials used for this and went and threw them into the evil forest. Then he tore out a yard from the piece of george cloth and hung it up like a flag at the shrine of the Sky god. He also left at the shrine the remaining forty nzu as well as four feathers which he plucked from the eagle. Then he scooped out a kolanut from the pod, broke it and began an invocation: "It is Omenŭkọ who is approaching you (the gods) for reunion. The things which he brought appeared satisfactory to me, nevertheless, I asked for your explicit confirmation. You manifested your concurrence by sending down the vultures to devour the sacrifice we had brought before you. Therefore, I urge you from today henceforth, to show your favor towards Omenŭkọ and his family." Then he broke a kolanut and offered it to Omenŭkọ and Igwe and the other people around. He also chewed some of the alligator pepper and spat out the pieces of the kolanut and the pepper on to his 'ofo', his ritual staff of authority. When these rituals were over, he set down the pot which had been boiling on the fire. The meat was cut up into pieces and shared to every individual present but not before some had been offered to the gods and ancestors. They ate and drank together, which symbolized that Omenŭkọ's reunion with the people, gods and ancestors had been consummated. While they continued drinking and chatting, Omenụkọ begged the chief priest to excuse his team for the night. They thanked and shook hands with each other warmly and Omenụkọ and his companions retired to his friend, Igwe's house to pass the night.

The next day, Omenụkọ told Igwe that it was time for him to go home and he urged Igwe to come and see him as soon as possible so that they could relax and review their recent experience. Igwe agreed and then Omenụkọ embarked on his journey home. When he reached home, he assembled all his brothers and narrated to them how things went. They were exceedingly happy. A few days later, Omenụkọ called together everybody in his residence, and told them about his reunion with his people adding: "Let us reflect on our homeland as we move about day and night, whoever wants to visit our town now is free to do so. Anyone who wants to marry from our town can do so now. If any young men from our town approach any of us to marry our daughters, we should give our consent if we are satisfied with their family backgrounds. I am now reconciled with our people, gods and ancestors. Again, it was my intention to ransom *all* the young men I sold but I could not. Of the two that I couldn't ransom, one called Oti had been dead for some time now. The other, who was one of my carriers, could not be traced. He must have been sold again into a distant land. I could be blamed for these but after the reunion with our people, I don't think that will be the case again. I told the family of the man that couldn't be traced that if he could be found anywhere, I shall not fail to do whatever it takes to ransom him too. I must assure you that I am happier and more at ease now than I have ever been since the day I fled our town. If death comes to me now, I shall not be afraid because there won't be so much I would have to confess before I breathe my last. This is all I have to say to you all. Please rejoice with me."

CHAPTER ELEVEN
Omenụkọ and His Brothers Rebuild their Compound

Omenụkọ had a lot of property and was a very prosperous man. He was the type of person anyone would know at first sight that he was truly a great man. He had a lot of money. He had several wives. He had very many children, both boys and girls. There were also his three brothers and their wives and children as well as his cousin Obioha all of whom were part of his large extended family. All of them were also great because they came to be just as wealthy and famous as Omenụkọ. Altogether, they were regarded as a town in themselves, as they had a chief like other towns did, and that chief was Omenụkọ.

Omenụkọ began to build houses for his large family. The structure of the houses would amaze anyone by its beauty and magnificence.

First, he built a wall around the compound. There were five sections of the compound for the five brothers, and all the houses were situated on five divisions, so that even though they were separate quarters, they were all within the same compound. Hedges were planted around the compound and along footpaths within the compound. Omenụkọ's own house could be called "House A", Okorafo's "House B", Nwabueze's "House C", Ogbonnaya's "House D", while Obioha's was "House E." The houses in Omenụkọ's section were four. The first one was for his sons. The second adjacent to the first belonged to his wives, and then there were two big houses which were exclusively for Omenụkọ himself. One served as his sitting and reception place and the other as his sleeping place. Omenụkọ moved from house to house. One month, he would use a house for sitting and reception, the next month he would convert it into a sleeping place and so on. He was truly comfortable and happy with himself.

It was difficult for an outsider to know the exact number of Omenụkọ's wives judging from the large number of children of both sexes that his wives bore him. His three brothers too, had several wives each and also many, many, children. Even though Omenụkọ had numerous wives, he took care of all of them and was genuinely devoted to all of them. In fact, he was as devoted to all of them as a husband with just one wife could be expected to be. And because of this, he was in harmony with his wives and his entire family.

When the buildings were completed, at his Ikpa Oyi residence, Omenụkọ went to his home town and married three wives for Obioha. After this, he sent for all the chiefs in and around Mgborogwu to come and see his new quarters. Perhaps because of his wealth, people might think that those houses would be roofed with zinc or corrugated iron sheets, but no, they were all mud houses with thatched roofs.

When the chiefs arrived on the appointed day, Omenụkọ served them kola and then showed them around his premises. There were forty-five chiefs altogether and what they saw amazed them greatly. Each of them congratulated him and also gave him a present. Some gave him one pound, others fifteen shillings and others ten shillings. Nobody gave anything more than one pound and no one gave anything less than ten shillings. When Omenụkọ had received these gifts, he thanked them very much. He was quite flattered by their generosity because he was not expecting anything from them. Next he entertained them. He had killed one cow and one goat purposely for the occasion. He used the goat meat exclusively for pepper-soup dish but the beef was cut into chunks and cooked separately. The chiefs took home large portions of food and meat.

Shortly afterwards, Omenuko also invited the chiefs from his home town, to come and 'see' his new quarters. The chiefs already had a custom about such things and so they readily obliged. Each person brought a gift for Omenuko. When they saw the houses, they were very pleased and praised Omenuko calling him 'Dimkpa', a mighty man! After Omenuko had entertained them with food and drinks, they presented their gifts to him. Most of them gave him a pound and the rest gave him fifteen shillings each. Omenuko thanked them very much and went into his room and brought out portions of the cow he had killed and cooked and presented them for distribution as he did with the chiefs that visited earlier. The chiefs were very jubilant and greeted him with a new praise-name: a fitting extension of his name, "Omenuko Aku, Omenuko–Aku!!" (one whose generosity is most evident at a time of scarcity). They continued eating and drinking until very late at night. They slept there and continued merry-making the next morning with a sumptuous breakfast after which they thanked Omenuko and then went home.

CHAPTER TWELVE
Omenụkọ's Wealth Attracts Jealousy

Omenụkọ continued to prosper in everything he put his hand to. The Whiteman did not fail to recognize his astute wisdom and uncommon abilities. So Omenụkọ was appointed "Paramount Chief," the highest rank in Warrant chieftaincy. He was also given the right to hold court and try certain cases at his residence. He did so well in these matters that the Whiteman assigned him more powers and more cases. They assigned a court clerk and some other support staff to him. All these meant that all the other chiefs in the land were now under Omenụkọ's supervision.

The chiefs in Mgborogwu and surrounding communities resented this and began grumbling among themselves: "We can never allow this to happen in our own land, that one who is after all, a stranger should be our executive head and overseer. If they intend him to be the Government itself, he should go and be that in his homeland, not on our soil." Although he had made peace with his people Omenụkọ was still living at "Ikpa Oyi;" He was yet to return to the land where he was born. These chiefs, therefore, started being mean to Omenụkọ to force him out of their territory. They sent a delegation to the Whiteman at Awka to express their opposition to Omenụkọ's continuation in office as Paramount chief, on the grounds that he was a stranger in their land. But the Whiteman ignored their protest because Omenụkọ was a chief with an impeccable character and high sense of justice; no one could deny that. When the chiefs saw that they did not sound convincing enough to the Whiteman, they retreated for the time being, to give thought on how they could obtain their demands, if possible by force. But while they waited, Omenụkọ grew more prosperous and the chiefs became more resentful of him. When some of the people saw that Omenụkọ was not reacting in any retaliatory manner to the twenty-five malicious chiefs, they began to feel favorably inclined again towards him and definitely sought his friendship. These people were sincere, and fortunately Omenụkọ accepted their offer of friendship. It would have been very sad if he had turned them down because they would have felt terribly let down. Thus people who wanted to cultivate Omenụkọ's friendship always went to his house and performed little unsolicited household tasks for him. The men cleared bushes for his farming and planted crops, while their wives did the weeding, and tending of the crops. When the walls surrounding Omenụkọ's compound needed repair, the men again came and offered their services. When there were leaks in the roofs of his houses, they came and did all the repairs necessary. This state of affairs continued for the next seven or eight years. And then the jealous chiefs rose again! They went to the chief who was the owner of the land, part of which was the site that Omenụkọ and his brothers cleared and built their new houses on. They urged him to ask Omenụkọ to vacate his land. He declined their request, unless they first swore an oath that once he had begun the process of ejecting Omenụkọ from the land, none of the chiefs would turn around to betray him. They all swore to this asking the gods to kill whoever relaxes in their determination to get rid of Omenụkọ. Next, they all escorted this chief to go and complain to the District Commissioner that the land where Omenụkọ built his compound was the chief's, and that he had asked Omenụkọ to vacate his land, but Omenụkọ had given deaf ear to his demands. "I have appealed to him peacefully without success. I have spoken to him in harsh tones and he was not moved. So please, it could be he does not understand Igbo; would you be kind enough to address him in English for me? Perhaps he would be able to understand and vacate my property." The District Commissioner cross-examined the chief:

"How long has Omenụkọ lived on your property?"

"This year will be the eighth year."

"In the past seven years and until today, how many times have you given him notice to vacate your property?"

"I have never told him to vacate my property but I have asked him to pay rent for the land and he has never complied."

"I thought you said a little while ago that you had appealed to him peacefully and in harsh tones to leave your land, and he only turned deaf ears to your demands? How do I reconcile this with your last statement? Which of the two is a fact?"

"The first one, sir."

"So the latter statement was a lie?"

"Yes, sir."

"I believe you often convict perjurers in your court, don't you?"

"Sir, please forgive me this first offense; I shall never lie again."

"Okay, I will forgive you but remember this: you made two statements, one of which you have now retracted as a lie. I shall not be pleased when eventually Omenụkọ stands in the witness box with you, to discover that all your statements today are false. In that case, you know very well, that you will serve a prison sentence for perjury."

"But sir, Omenụkọ is a great orator. He could use this to my disadvantage when he comes here. He may falsely deny what I say, and still appear to be speaking the truth before your eyes. You will then condemn me as a liar. As my people say, rather than accept invitation to a feast and die on the road, I stay hungry."

"What does that last part mean?"

"It means, I have decided not to go further with the case against Omenụkọ. He is very clever and no matter what happens, he will deny everything I say when the time comes."

The District Commissioner dismissed the chiefs and asked them to go and think over the whole issue and when they had thoroughly considered it, they should come and tell him the truth. He waited for several days, but they never showed up again. So one day the District Commissioner sent for Omenụkọ to come and see him. He also sent for that chief who accused Omenụkọ to come and see him on the same day. When both of them arrived and stood before him, he asked them if they had any dispute between them. Omenụkọ replied that he knew of no personal dispute between Chief Ike and himself except that all the surrounding chiefs had risen against him for no just cause. The District Commissioner then addressed Chief Ike: "What is your answer to my question?" He replied, "There is no dispute between Chief Omenụkọ and me, sir." "I see," said the District Commissioner. "Has he then vacated your property?" Chief Ike was evasive in his reply. "Oh, that matter? You can forget it, Master, it is all over." But the District Commissioner asked Omenụkọ pointedly whether Chief Ike had at any time spoken to him about that piece of land on which he built his new residence. Omenụkọ answered: "Never, not for once, sir." Then the District Commissioner asked them to go. They left but Omenụkọ continued to reflect on those questions that the District Commissioner asked both he and Chief Ike. There were only questions and no explanations. This very much baffled Omenụkọ, so he went back to the District Commissioner some days later and asked for explanations. "I couldn't make head or tail of those questions you put before us, and they have bothered my mind since that day." "Well, if you are desirous to know, I have to tell you because I have known your character for some time. Since the whole story had no basis in fact, I trust you would not pursue it further in anyway. I asked those questions because previously Ike and the other chiefs had come here to lodge a *false* complaint before me, that the land on which you built your compound belonged to Ike and that Ike had been appealing to you to vacate from his property, but you disregarded his pleas. So Ike appealed to me to speak to you in

English, for that might be the language that you understand better. He was taking the action because you had even refused to pay the rent charged you on the land. I found out that he was lying and gave him time to go and think it over and then come back and tell me the truth, but he never showed up again. That was why I sent for both of you together and asked those questions. And you heard his answers, asking me to forget the matter for 'it was over'. So according to him, I must regard the matter as closed." Omenụkọ said to the District Commissioner, "You are like a door between my people and me. You see what happens inside the room and also what happens outside. You see all the reports of our individual court cases and the judgments we deliver. You know our strengths and our individual weaknesses. Well, since you have asked me to drop the matter, I shall do so. Thank you". And he left.

When Omenụkọ reached home, he called together all his people and told them all that transpired. He told them that there was nothing to worry about, it was mere gossip designed by the other chiefs to upset him. He added: "I owe nothing to anyone either in this land or in our homeland. The only obligations I owe to people are those coming from a charitable disposition and a gracious heart, because God had enriched me in various ways. If anyone said that I was poor and downcast and lost my self-respect when I sold the children of other people, the person might be right. But no one among these chiefs can say that his son was among those children that I sold, to justify a vengeance. I tell you, we would have gone back to our homeland, if the Whiteman had so suggested because in my mind, I don't see anything that these chiefs could do to me. Rather if I am no more today, things might be worse for them than they could ever imagine."

When his family had listened to all this, they were of the opinion that they should all go back to their homeland rather than be victims of envy and prejudice where they were. Meanwhile, Omenụkọ asked them to simply prepare their minds that they would eventually have to go home. Omenụkọ's wealth and popularity continued to increase by leaps and bounds. The Government continued to appreciate his judicial activities and his high sense of responsibility even as the chiefs continued to nurse implacable hatred towards him.

CHAPTER THIRTEEN
The Last Straw

Twenty-six towns allied themselves together to persecute Omenụkọ. They made a resolution to draw him into an open physical combat. They were determined to bear the consequences of their rash conduct, even if that meant death for them. But one thing was certain, they must pitch battle against Omenụkọ and his people! But some of the people in the group had serious doubts about the success of such a confrontation. They were not sure how many people were on Omenụkọ's side and they feared to be beaten. These men, therefore, sneaked out and revealed to Omenụkọ what was about to happen. Their major belief in divulging the secret to Omenụkọ was so that he could draw the attention of the Government to the planned attack. The Government would then step in to avoid a bloodshed. But little did they realize how strong-willed Omenụkọ and his people were and that, in fact, they would opt to wage a war with twenty-six towns! Omenụkọ called all his people together and said to them: "We must fight these people, if indeed they come. There is one thing we must know beforehand. If we fight, the Whiteman would be very disappointed with me. But we must fight because we are being attacked in our home. That is self-defense. This is not like a war that is formally declared in which people would blame me for being in it. But this is a battle for survival and self-preservation. Our enemies are swooping down on us to wipe us out. We must, therefore, defend ourselves. I know very well that once this battle is fought, we have no choice but to leave this land."

So Omenụkọ and his people armed themselves to the teeth and stood waiting. On the day that the twenty-six towns had embarked for the attack, they approached and began by destroying all the crops and vegetables in Omenụkọ's farms and gardens. Then Omenụkọ ordered his people to open fire. "Let it happen now!" They opened fire on the intruders. One man was struck dead on the spot and several others were wounded. The intruders returned fire and also shot to death one member of Omenụkọ's group. So far the casualties were balanced. Both sides took the deceased from their camp and went to Awka to make a formal report to the District Commissioner. The District Commissioner saw the corpses and asked them for explanations. Omenụkọ was the first to speak: "Sir, please ask twenty-six towns why they conspired and resolved that they would never rest until they have vanquished me and my people. As a result of that resolution in a meeting which they held, they surged into my compound today to attack us. When my people tried to prevent their entry they killed one of my people on the spot and contrived to carry away his corpse, so that it could not be proved that they killed any of my men. But their malicious actions did not stop at that. They destroyed all the crops and vegetables in my farms and gardens. Nobody from my house tried to prevent them or show any opposition until they moved from the farms and actually struck at my living quarters. That was the time that they killed my man because my people had specifically tried to defend our compound. At that outrage, I asked my people to return an eye for an eye and so my people too, killed one of their men, after which they retreated. The chiefs had come without guns, so when they heard the gun shot and saw that one of their men was already dead, they all fled. Those among them, who were carrying the corpse of the man they had killed from my family, thrust the corpse aside and ran away when they saw that their people had taken to their heels. So we recovered the corpse. But in their haste, they also omitted to carry the corpse of their own man. There were three people among them whom we had taken as prisoners. However, we released them and made them carry the corpse right back to their people. One more thing, I would like you to ask the court clerk and other court officials to check my files and declare openly my citizenship." The District Commissioner asked the twenty-six towns what they had to say. Were Omenuko's statements true or false? They pointed out that some were true and some false. The District Commissioner asked them to be specific. They replied that they had asked Omenuko to return to his homeland. The District Commissioner ruled the answer out of order, saying it had no bearing whatsoever on the material question. "Now listen, and answer this!", he ordered them. "Did you break into Omenuko's compound or did you not?" They denied ever breaking into his compound but they admitted that they had destroyed some cash crops in his farm—some cocoa trees, plantains, and a few others. They told the District Commissioner that it was at that point, that Omenuko and his people fired guns at them and killed their comrade. The District Commissioner then asked, "Do you realize that you are guilty for provoking the fight?" "Yes, indeed," they replied. The District Commissioner put another question to them: "Do you know what this could mean for you?" And they replied that they were ready for the consequences. "We will be prepared to listen to the law, only when we have killed Omenuko. If you want to execute all of us, because of a stranger who came into our midst, we would prefer to die, rather than allow our eyes to see our ears." The District Commissioner was shocked at all of their utterances made remorselessly with impunity. He ordered both sides to go and bury the corpses and report back in four days' time.

The following day, the District Commissioner sent a policeman to go and bring Omenuko to the court. He came back to Awka the same day with Omenuko. The District Commissioner spoke to Omenuko in private and because he wanted to get the facts of the case, he said to Omenuko, "Tell me the truth about the allegations of these people. They persist in saying that you are a stranger in their land and that indeed your original home is in Okigwe." Omenụkọ answered: "I cannot lie to you. I come from a town in Okigwe as they said." The District Commissioner was at a loss what to tell Omenụkọ without necessarily upsetting him. "What actually infuriates me in the situation is that twenty-six towns should rise against one man. You never can say to what extent they would go in their hunt for your life. They could get a reckless die-hard to go after your life and stop at nothing until he assassinates you. What would be my choice but to execute just that one man, in all probability, a good-for-nothing person, and he would not even deny the murder? He would look upon himself as a hero, and that makes it more painful for me. Therefore, I must advise you to prepare and go back to your hometown. Your fame has spread far and wide down to Okigwe and beyond. I have found no fault in you whatsoever to warrant denying you your title and status wherever you might be."

Omenụkọ took a hard line and asked the District Commissioner: "What punishment would you mete out to them for persecuting and attacking me in my own house? If they are not severely punished for this, there is no knowing what they might be trying next. As for me, I shall start this day to pack my things. I would also send for my people to come and carry home my belongings. Let me assure you that I owe nothing to anybody in my homeland and, therefore, have no fear about going home." The District Commissioner asked Omenụkọ to inform him whenever he was ready to leave finally for his home. Omenụkọ thanked him and went back and told his people all that the District Commissioner had said. They rejoiced saying, "Better to go home alive than be carried home dead." Omenụkọ said to them: "We have to go. A man who goes into a fight has to consider in detail what he stands to gain by fighting. In the present situation, I do not think I stand to gain anything from this fight. I don't see what they themselves would gain either. Let them eat their land when we have gone."

CHAPTER FOURTEEN
Omenụkọ's Homecoming

Omenụkọ sent eight people to go and tell the chiefs of his hometown what he had been going through. There were fifteen villages and each had a chief. Omenụkọ requested each of the chiefs to send him carriers to help facilitate his movement back home. All the chiefs responded immediately. A message was passed round all the villages by town criers asking young men to hurry down to Omenụkọ's residence at Ikpa Oyi the next morning to help him and his brothers carry home their belongings. The task would continue until everything belonging to Omenụkọ's family had been brought home. After this the chiefs set the stage for festivities with drummers and musicians performing continuously to herald Omenụkọ's homecoming. Everywhere the sound of the drums was heard: "kpo kpa; kpo kpa." The following day all the roads were filled with people—men, women and children alike. They could have crushed anyone on the road with their mere footsteps. It took nine days to bring home everything that Omenụkọ and his people possessed. On the tenth day, Omenụkọ went and told the District Commissioner that he was ready to go home. "Well," said the District Commissioner, "but what about your people and your things?" Omenụkọ assured him that all his things had been carried home. Then the District Commissioner asked him what he intended to do with his houses. Omenụkọ answered that he would leave them to rot away, decay, and fall down. "No!" protested the District Commissioner. "Those houses should never be allowed to come to waste. They are much too valuable for that." But Omenụkọ was unyielding. "There are a lot of things I shall have to give away to my friends but not those houses." The District Commissioner expressed regret that Omenụkọ should allow those houses to come to ruins. He suggested to Omenụkọ at least to sell the houses to his friends. Omenụkọ definitely refused saying: "If I find anyone in that compound, I will deal very seriously with that person. When the houses have all crumbled and become waste, whoever wishes can go and live there. But for now, my answer is no." The District Commissioner said no more about the houses. Rather, he told Omenụkọ that when he had settled down properly in his hometown, and wished to return to his judicial duties, he should come back to Awka and pick up a letter of introduction to present to the District Commissioner in charge of Okigwe. Omenụkọ told him that he would come but that it might not be within the next year or two. He explained that anyone who was going into chieftaincy duties should first build proper houses where his fellow chiefs could feel comfortable if they chose to visit him at any time. The District Commissioner did not object. He and Omenụkọ shook hands and wished each other well, and then Omenụkọ left.

The day before his final exit, Omenụkọ brought out four cannons that he had and loaded them well. He had them lined up on top of a hill and he appointed sixteen strong men to stand by, so that when the guns had been fired, they would carry the empty guns home, as the last of his things to be brought home. At the exact hour of his departure, he ordered the cannons to be fired. One of the sixteen men touched off each of the guns with a little flame and they went off booming in quick succession. Omenụkọ told people who were standing by that the purpose of firing the loaded guns was to alert the Mgborogwu people that he was about to depart from their land. In that case his enemies might rejoice to their hearts' content while those who cared to weep for his departure would know when to begin doing so. After that explanation, the sixteen men carried the empty cannons and together with Omenuko, they set off for home. When Omenuko reached home, again he fired four cannons to report his arrival to his people.

No one can say exactly the year Omenuko fled from his homeland to Mgborogwu, but he returned towards the end of October in 1918.

After Omenuko had stayed for quite a while without going to the District Commissioner to pick up his Warrant, many people began to get concerned. They approached him to find out what could possibly be wrong. Omenuko explained to them that he had no great desire to continue as a Warrant chief anymore, but he would always be ready to cooperate with government whenever they sought his advice or services. His people were not at all pleased to hear this. They could not bring themselves to imagine that Omenuko would give up the office of a "Paramount Chief", a post that the Whiteman himself judged him fit for. But Omenuko had definitely resolved to retire from the court and gave his reason to his people this way: "I have been a Paramount Chief for some time. People saw my performances and praised me. Now I want to be an honorary peacemaker representing the Government in my town. That is all I want to do now and I believe it will be of mutual benefit to my community and me." And so it was that Omenuko voluntarily retired from the court, just as he said.

CHAPTER FIFTEEN
Omenụkọ's Life in His Hometown

Omenụkọ built many houses for his entire family. He also sent his male children to school. But there were many already who were completing their final year in school just before their homecoming. There were many also who had already finished their primary school before their return. But since that year (1918) when they came back, there was no year when one or two of his sons, did not complete primary education. Every year too, at least one of his sons was sure to join the Whiteman's civil service in such capacities as court clerks, law enforcement officers, and so on. Many of his children also went into transport business and many took to trading.

Omenụkọ continued to go to the courts as an interested observer. He watched every proceeding scrupulously and frowned seriously whenever the chiefs or the judges erred. Therefore, whenever he was in court, the court officials paid extra attention to their behavior and their pronouncements.

However, human beings being what they are, not all of the people loved or appreciated Omenụkọ. There were people who always liked to sponge on others but never shared anything of their own with anyone else. Omenụkọ could not please all of the people all the time. Consequently, some admired him and some hated him. But any fair-minded person would admit that by all standards

Omenụkọ was really a man of the people, and for that alone his friends outnumbered his detractors in his hometown.

EPILOGUE

I have written this book about the life of Mazi Omenụkọ so that anyone who reads it may have something to learn from his life. The way in which life is a mixture of joy and sorrow, hardship and reward, laughter and tears, is in itself, enough lesson for anyone who seeks to learn. Omenụkọ became rich at an early age. When he became a grown man, his wealth eluded him. Sorrow and disillusionment counseled him to kill himself and take a rest from all the vicissitudes of life, but peace and happiness counseled him to be patient and look towards the future. Omenụkọ obeyed and stayed alive. He continued to perform the good acts of his life. Whenever he decided to do anything, he would wait for the most opportune moment. The correctness of his instinct was a vindication of his wisdom and expert judgment. Everybody is aware how scarce money is these days. Since 1929, some people have as it were, chained their money with rope and hoarded it securely in self-provided vaults. They have maintained a tight grip on their money to avoid its escape. Omenụkọ happens to be one of those people. Many people today cry about the scarcity of money, but Omenụkọ seems to be waiting, as I know him to do always, for the opportune time to manifest his economic wisdom. There is scarcity of money everywhere now, but Omenụkọ is as his name implies, one who acts during a period of scarcity. That was the name given to him by his parents and Omenụkọ has lived up to it in every way. It is no wonder, therefore, that he should in these years of depression, begin to set up a storey building, a vindication of the foresight of his father who named him: "O Me N'uko Aku" One who acts during a period of scarcity—one whose affluence is most evident at a time of scarcity and need. Omenụkọ lived and acted true to his name!

Printed in the United States
By Bookmasters